INFECTION Z 4

RYAN CASEY

The characters and events portrayed in this book are fictitious. Any similarity to real persons, living or dead, is coincidental and not intended by the author. Any reference to real locations is only for atmospheric effect, and in no way truly represents those locations.

Copyright © 2015 by Ryan Casey

Cover design by Cormar Creative

All rights reserved.

No part of this book may be reproduced in any form or by any electronic or mechanical means, including information storage and retrieval systems, without written permission from the author, except for the use of brief quotations in a book review.

Published by Higher Bank Books

If you want to be notified when Ryan Casey's next novel is released and receive an exclusive free book from his Dead Days post apocalyptic series, please sign up to his mailing list.

http://ryancaseybooks.com/fanclub

Your email address will never be shared and you can unsubscribe at any time.

INFECTION Z: 4

CHAPTER ONE

"We need to get the hell away from this place. Quick!"

Ella Williams sprinted as fast as she could up the slippery muddy slope. Rain lashed down from the thick, grey April clouds. Winter was constant, never loosening its grip even into spring. Felt like the infection had ravaged the world forever when really it had only been a matter of months.

A matter of months where Ella had done more running, more fleeing, more surviving, than her entire life prior combined.

She looked back at the rest of her group. Saw them clambering their way up the side of the hill. Covered in mud, soaked in rain. She could hear their panting. The pained grunts of people struggling to survive. Of people doing everything they could to make it in an unforgiving world.

And Ella knew how it was. They'd been pushed to their limits. All of them had been pushed to their limits.

Not for much longer.

Not now they had a destination in mind.

Ella tried not to look behind her twenty-nine strong group at the figures drifting closer. Gave her a sickly taste in her mouth just glancing at them. Their greying skin. The inevitable wounds on their bodies. They never got any less scary, any less intimidating. Didn't matter how many of them you fought off, how many of their sharp, snapping teeth you slipped away from, they remained terrifying. A constant reminder of what you'd become—of what everyone would become—if you just made one slip...

Ella saw Michael slip the moment she had the thought.

Saw him tumble down the hill, roll in the mud.

Towards the figures.

Her first instinct was to run back down. To go down there and save him. And that's what she wanted to do. Put her life on the line. Put everything on the line. That's what she was supposed to do for other people. For *her* people.

But Michael was falling fast.

Screaming as he plummeted down towards the silhouettes.

The rest of the group just watching as he rolled away.

The desire to survive glowing in their eyes.

"What—what do we—"

Margaret didn't finish her question.

She slipped too.

Slipped down the muddy hill, down towards the dead.

Just as she started to roll, Ella heard Michael's scream.

She winced. Turned away. She didn't want to watch him get torn to pieces. She'd spoken to him just earlier that day. Spoken about the usual—life before, family, wife, kids. What they were both going to do when all this ended.

When all this ended...

Ella knew how much of a farce that notion was now.

As the sound of Michael's muscles being ripped from his bones resounded around the hillside, Ella knew exactly how much of a farce any hope was.

Unless...

"Ella," Natasha called. She was a pretty girl with dark hair, gorgeous Malaysian features. Always looked good, even in the midst of the apocalypse. "We—we can't just leave them. We can't just walk away."

Ella was about to respond when Margaret's screams filled the air. The wind blew rain into Ella's face. She swore she smelled rusty metal.

Blood.

She wiped at the corners of her eyes. Kept herself steady, nearing the top of the hill. "We're so close."

"But we can't just walk on."

"We don't have a choice," Ella said. "Not anymore."

Ella saw the look in Natasha's eyes. The look she'd seen many times before. She knew what it was. Natasha didn't like her methods. She didn't like that Ella made the tough decisions. She didn't understand the bigger picture: that sometimes members of a group had to die for the larger group to survive.

That's the way the world was now. That's how it worked.

That's how it'd always worked.

"Now come on," Ella said, turning around and beginning her ascent of the hill once more. She stuck her nails in the dirt, dragged her body up. She'd heard about what was up the hill. Heard a group back in Wolverhampton discussing the other side.

She heard what they said, and she knew she had to reach this place. She knew she had to see it for herself.

And she knew everyone would have to see it for themselves if they'd heard what Ella heard.

If everyone heard what Ella heard, they'd understand why she had to make tough decisions. Why she had to leave people to die. Why she had to—

Snap.

The cracking of a bone. Margaret's or Michael's.

She tried not to remember the humans they once were. Tried not to consider the *things* they'd become.

Just remember them positively. Remember them as they were before. Michael and his jokes. Margaret and her cute complaining.

Remember them as they were.

Remember them as they—

Another noise. This time, slurping. Like guts being sucked out of a carcass.

Ella tried to block out the burning taste of sick building behind her lips.

Just a few metres to the top of the hill.

A few metres left to struggle before seeing the truth.

Seeing what was on the other side.

Seeing...

She felt her left hand slip away. But before she could react, before she could even think to clutch at the ground, she was falling. Rolling down the mud. Everything too slippery to get hold of. Nothing to reach for.

"Help!"

She screamed, got a mouthful of mud. A part of her hoped she bumped into one of her companions. That they softened her fall. Okay, maybe they'd fall too if that was the case, but again, sometimes people just had to die to save the wider group.

She was okay with that now.

She'd come to terms with it.

Accepted it.

But nobody was there to cushion her.

Just the long roll down the hill.

The long roll in the mud. The rain.

Towards...

She stopped. Stopped, right in a ditch near the bottom of the hill. Her head spun. Heart raced. She was unbalanced. Disoriented. Lost all sense of which direction she'd even rolled down from.

Then she saw her group. Saw them at the top of the hill. Billy. Dinesh. Miriam. All of them standing there in the rain. All of them staring out at something.

Staring out at *it*.

The other side.

"Is it there?" Ella screamed. She just wanted them to turn around. Just wanted them to tell her whether it was there. She just wanted to know.

Footsteps approached from Ella's left.

She didn't turn to look at them. Didn't acknowledge the rotting smell. She just kept her focus on the top of the hill. More of her group reaching it. More of them standing there. Staring.

Not turning back for Ella.

Not telling her what they could see.

"Hey!" Ella screamed. "What is it? What—what do you see?"

She saw Natasha at the top of the hill. Saw her turn around. Look right down at her.

She saw that look in Natasha's eyes again.

Saw her open her mouth, prepare to speak.

And then she felt something.

A splitting, burning pain on her neck.

Then on her back, right through to the spine.

Then on her thighs.

Her ankles.

Her belly.

She felt the undead shove their filthy fingers inside the holes they'd bitten into her skin. Felt the canvas of her body splitting apart like tender pulled pork.

But still she looked up at her group.

Still, as they ripped out her insides, as blood curdled in her throat, as the sounds of her raw flesh being chewed up filled her ears, she kept on looking up at Natasha, looking at her people staring over the hill at something.

"What..." she started.

Then she felt teeth on her tongue.

Saw one of the undead above her. It looked into her eyes with its deathly stare.

Biting down, ripping her tongue away.

She started to cry. Started to cry as the undead tore her to shreds. Because she knew. She knew she'd never see the other side. She knew she'd never see whatever was over that hill.

Was it like the people back in Wolverhampton said?

Was their journey worth it?

Were their losses worth it?

She caught a glance of Natasha once more.

Only this time, she saw a smile twitching at the sides of Natasha's mouth.

She tried to call out for Natasha. For the rest of her group. She just wanted to know. Her final wish before she died, before she turned.

But then Natasha looked away.

And with the rest of the group, she started to walk.

As the undead swooped in for another helping of her flesh, Ella saw herself as if from above. She saw herself lying in the mud, rain lashing down, diluting her blood.

Alone.

And as she looked up at the sky, she saw the sun peeking through the clouds, felt its warmth touch her skin, and her insides —which were outsides now, she guessed.

She thought about the other side.

She hoped for the sake of her group they'd find what was promised there.

She took a final painful breath.

Then, she closed her eyes.

ELLA WOULD SEE what was on the other side of the hill. She'd see it very soon.

Only she wouldn't be human when she saw it.

CHAPTER TWO

Hayden McCall watched the house on the corner for hours.

He knew it was hours because he could feel his forehead burning in the sun. It was only April, but today had been good. Pleasant, as old folks used to say when killing time at bus stops. A really fucking pleasant day. Made a change.

It'd be even more pleasant if he saw no signs of life in this house.

The house he had to get inside.

The house he had to search for supplies.

The house he had to leave.

He lowered his binoculars. Looked at the empty street. Well, it wasn't exactly empty. Dusty cars. Smashed windows. Flies buzzing around remains. A constant smell that hung around every town, every village, every suburban area.

The smell that signalled *they* had been here.

They had been everywhere.

He stood up. Walked down the hill towards the road. There were lots of flies about. Way too many for April. There'd even been flies in the cold of winter. So much death that even the flies found a way to adapt to the changing temperatures.

If only people could adapt to change as well as flies.

He whistled as he climbed over the wooden fence at the bottom of the cul-de-sac. Made his way towards the white and black-beamed Victorian house. He kept on whistling, a little louder this time. If there were any undead around, he wanted to know. The zombies always seemed to approve of his singing. Always came wandering out whenever he broke out in melody.

Well, just a pity for their sakes they didn't stay inside.

Just a pity they didn't adapt.

Hearing no footsteps, hearing nothing at all but the buzzing of flies and the gentle breeze, he walked down the driveway of the old detached house. He'd chosen it because it looked like it once belonged to someone wealthy. And if there's one thing he'd learned since the world went to shit, it's that the wealthy kept a lot of interesting supplies. Food. Drinks. Stuff to kill time. Stuff to kill *things*.

And another good thing about the wealthy was that they were rarely still alive to try and stop him taking what was theirs.

They were just too weak.

Money couldn't buy survival. Not in this world. Not anymore.

Hayden tried turning the handle. Locked.

He crouched by the door and lifted the plant pot.

If there was another thing he'd learned since the world went to shit, it's that even the wealthy made the stupid mistake of leaving a spare key lying around outside.

He reached beneath the plant pot.

Felt cold metal against his fingertips.

"Bingo."

His voice sounded deeper than he remembered. Didn't speak much these days. Didn't have much to speak about, many people to speak with. He'd been alone for a while. Alone since the end of winter.

Alone since...

No.

He didn't want to think about the past.

Just the future.

Only the future.

He put the key in the lock. Turned it.

And then he lifted his hammer and lowered the handle of the door.

Movement.

Movement on the road to his left.

He swung around. Scanned the street.

Nothing.

Nothing but an old crisp packet floating in the wind.

Nothing but flies.

Nothing.

He held his breath and turned back to the door. Pushed it open.

First thing he did was the usual—took in a deep breath. Checked for smells. Listened out for any noise. Usually, noise was a better indicator that the dead were around. Sense of smell could get fucked up in a world like this. A world where your nostrils were treated to so much death.

Regardless, he didn't smell a thing in this house.

He didn't hear a thing, either.

Just the flies outside.

Just the crisp packet tapping against the pavement, dragged along by the breeze.

Hayden kept his hammer raised. Stepped inside what appeared to be a kitchen. It was dark and dusty. An ironing board lay across the black and white tiles, an unfinished T-shirt all crumpled up underneath it. Blackened bananas by the windowsill. A pool of water in front of the freezer.

Hayden swallowed a thickening lump in his throat as he walked further into the kitchen. His eyes honed in on stuff that could be useful. IKEA knife set. Bottled cooking oil. Rolling pin. Car keys.

All of them sparkling in his vision like clues on a point and click video game.

He just had to decide what to look at first. What was most important.

He walked over to the fridge. Felt the water from the defrosted freezer seeping through his shoes. Shoes. That's something he needed. New shoes. These Timberlands were split at the sides. Anyway, he was kind of fed up with them. Fancied a new look. Some brown chukka boots, maybe. Or even some fresh Converse.

Everywhere was a shop these days.

Just had to make sure there wasn't anyone else shopping there, too.

He pulled open the fridge door.

Flies buzzed out, bumped into his face. He wafted them away, the sourness from the fridge making him want to heave. Before he closed the fridge door, he spotted maggots crawling around the partly-closed lid of a bottle of milk. Lettuce gone brown. A few cartons of Capri-Sun.

He reached past the maggots and the rotting food and grabbed the Capri-Sun drinks.

Always came in handy.

He closed the door and heard footsteps to his left.

He turned.

Saw a shadow move beneath the inside kitchen door.

His chest tightened. *That* feeling overcame him. The one that made his head ache. That made his breathing difficult.

The sense that someone was there.

Someone was in the house with him.

But the same sense that told him no one was there.

That it was all just... in his head, somehow.

He didn't like that feeling.

He didn't like how insane it made him sound.

He had to believe there was something on the other side of the door. He had to get out of here. Leave.

He couldn't be proven wrong.

Or that really would make him crazy.

That really would—

He heard shuffling.

He felt his mouth dry up. Stood opposite the door.

There was something in there. Definitely something in there.

Or someone.

He put the Capri-Sun drinks to one side. Raised his hammer. Walked over to the door.

He put his ear right up to it. Listened for the shuffling noise again.

Nothing but silence.

Just the flies.

The crisp packet outside.

The maggots slowly dripping down from the roof of the fridge.

Nothing at all.

He lowered the hammer. Turned around.

Someone stood at the kitchen door.

A man.

Hayden saw his greying skin. Saw the wound on his right arm. A deep wound, the flesh torn right from his body.

He tightened his grip on the hammer. Looked at the Capri-Suns. Got ready to put the fucker down.

And then another figure appeared behind the man.

Then another.

Then another.

All of them covered in bite wounds.

All of them smelling like shit.

All of them walking towards him.

He dodged the grip of the first zombie. Swung the hammer into its balding head. Its skull cracked on contact. But he knew that wasn't enough. He needed to get the neck. Snap the neck in two.

More zombies piled through the door.

The air getting thicker with the stench of death.

The mumbled, pained cries of the creatures overriding all other sounds.

Hayden backed up to the kitchen door. His heart pounded. Too many of them. Way too many of them.

The Capri-Suns out of reach.

No way of getting to them.

He had to go.

He had to leave.

He had to get away.

Now.

He lowered the handle of the kitchen door. Slammed it shut. Ran out into the hallway.

First thing he noticed was just how dark it was.

Then just how smelly it was.

And then he noticed the emaciated zombies at the bottom of the stairs.

They just stood there at first. Stood there, as if they were sleeping. Like they'd given up all hope of finding a meal; of finding fresh meat.

When they saw Hayden, he swore their eyes illuminated.

He scooted back.

Ran in the direction of the kitchen.

The kitchen door caved in.

Zombies piled out of it, filled the corridor, trapped him.

He looked either side. More zombies coming down the stairs. Fuck, what was this? Some kind of zombie congregation?

He looked around the hallway as the zombies grew in number.

The lounge door.

Only option.

Only choice.

He grabbed it. Turned the handle.

Stuck.

"Fuck."

He felt the cold bodies of the zombies closing in. Tried the handle again. Still so tight, like it hadn't been turned in months. Something behind it, too. Something blocking his entrance.

He kept on turning it.

Turning and turning as the zombies closed in.

Turning, pushing, doing everything he could to get inside.

He swung the hammer at the neck of the first zombie to approach from the left. Heard its spine crack, watched the zombie shake like it was having some kind of seizure.

Then he squared up to the door.

Pulled back the hammer.

Bashed it in, blow after blow after blow.

He watched the wood split away. Saw an armchair pressed up to the door. Fuck. Someone was in there. Or someone *had* been in there. The wealthy. Using their frigging expensive furniture to survive. If only they knew their acquisitions couldn't solve everything.

Hayden swung at another zombie. A girl, much younger than him. He tried not to see her as a girl. Tried to distance himself as the heavy head of the hammer shattered the bones in her neck. You couldn't get attached. You just couldn't. Not to the dead. Not to the living. Not anymore.

You just had to survive.

He smashed the door in some more. A large hole formed in the wood. He reached through it. Struggled to grab the handle, to turn whatever shitty lock was stopping his entrance.

Couldn't reach it.

Couldn't twist his arm enough.

He looked at the gathering zombies. Looked at them

surrounding him. Snarling. Blood and flesh drooling from their utterly inhuman mouths.

He didn't have long.

Seconds, if he was lucky.

So he turned to the opening.

Threw himself into it.

Landed face first on the armchair.

He felt the wood from the smashed door scratch his belly, splinter his arms. But even worse, he felt the pressure on his feet. Felt the pulling.

Felt the teeth sinking into his Timberlands.

He kicked back. Kicked back as hard as he could. Twisted, turned, shook like some kind of feral animal.

Because that's what he was. That's what he had to be to survive.

The humane didn't survive.

The diplomats rotted.

Democracy festered in a pit of filth.

He kicked again.

Swung free of the zombies.

Turned over, smacked the hammer right on the back of the neck of the final culprit.

And then he rolled off the armchair.

Ran over to the window.

"Sorry about this."

He pulled back his hammer.

Whacked it at the glass.

Smashed it on first contact.

He climbed out the window just as the first few zombies forced themselves into the lounge, no care at all for the way the wood tore up their bodies, no care about anything but meat. Human meat.

Hayden ran down the street, past stray zombies, back towards the hill.

When he glanced at the house, he swore he saw someone in the upstairs bedroom window.

A child.

A skinny, starving child with tears rolling down his cheeks.

The child stared at Hayden.

Lifted a hand to the glass.

Then his little neck exploded and blood covered the window.

"No!"

Hayden closed his eyes.

Eased his thoughts.

When he looked back at the house, the little boy was gone.

There was no blood on the window.

CHAPTER THREE

Hayden kept as quiet as he could as he approached the churchyard.

It was a nice spot just outside a small town. One of those proper traditional churches—all grey brick and moss. The graveyard wasn't bustling, either, but there was a sense that the headstones were gradually filling the land. Hayden thought about the concerns they must've had at the church. The worries about what to do when it just got too full.

At least they didn't have to worry about that anymore.

He twirled a daisy between his fingers as he perched outside the churchyard. He waited for a sound. Or a smell. Or sight of someone. He'd seen a couple of people around this spot a few days back. They had guns, and one of them fired at a headstone. He didn't want to mix with people like that. They were the last kind he wanted to deal with.

Not that he wanted to deal with anyone at all.

Better to just stay alone.

That way, he couldn't let anyone down.

He started to stand. The rain had eased, but the clouds were still thick. Soon, night would fall. Not as soon as it did in winter.

Hayden thought he was looking forward to the longer days. Increased visibility, less time to worry about what he couldn't see. Now, he wasn't so sure. Spend long enough in the darkness and it becomes your friend. Your greatest ally.

He saw the sun slowly setting and prayed for dark.

When darkness finally did arrive and still no sign of anybody —or anything—around the churchyard, he stepped inside. He ignored the silhouettes he thought he saw in the corners of his eyes. Had to adjust. Had to accept them for what they were— tricks, nothing more. The fantasies of a lonely mind. The projections of a messed up imagination.

He ignored them. Because there was no smell. There were no flies.

He was alone.

He had to be alone.

He walked over to the unmarked headstone right at the back of the graveyard. Somewhere above, an owl hooted, like the most stereotypical graveyard movie scene imaginable. The moon was bright behind the clouds. A little too bright for comfort.

But he was okay. He was okay because he was alone.

Alone with her.

Alone with Sarah.

He put the daisy by the side of the headstone. "Hello, Sarah." He wasn't sure why exactly he used this place as Sarah's grave. But since she'd fallen to her death over the Holyhead cliffside, after having no opportunity to stick around and commemorate her after the cliffside became infested by undead, he'd taken comfort in having *somewhere* to visit her. Just some place where he could stop by. Show he cared.

He was a long way from home. A long way from anyone.

But having Sarah here—having something to remember Sarah by—that made a difference.

It made him feel like he had someone to care for.

It made him feel less alone.

Slightly.

"Saw him again today," Hayden muttered. He looked around at the thick trees surrounding the graveyard. He wasn't sure he wanted to talk about what he'd seen. The boy in the window. Wasn't sure he wanted to let it all out. Not again.

But somehow, he found himself shaking.

Found the words spilling out.

"It's... it's like he's punishing me." He smiled. Shook his head. "What am I saying? Not 'him' exactly. But my mind. It's like my mind's punishing me. For what I did."

He stroked the top of the headstone. Felt his arms tingling as theory replayed in his mind, over and over and over.

The house.

The scream.

The look on the boy's face as Hayden ran from the window...

No.

No more.

Forget.

"It's... it's like no matter what I do, no matter where I go, I'll always remember. And maybe that's right. Maybe it's the way it should be. Because I know what I did. I—I have to live with what I did. I just can't..."

He refocused on the headstone. Perfect silence in the graveyard. The headstone saying nothing.

He smiled again. "What am I doing talking to the headstone of someone I don't even know?"

He said those words, but he knew exactly why. His memories constantly reminded him why.

He'd let Sarah die.

Let Newbie die.

Let...

"No!" he said, the tingling sensations building inside his skull. "That's not how it was. I didn't leave anyone."

You left them.

"Okay maybe I left them but—"

Aren't fit to lead anybody, nobody at all.

"I don't want to lead anyone. I don't—"

You let the little boy die watched him bleed watched him—

"NO!"

Hayden heard his shout echo around the churchyard. He heard shuffling in the hedgerows. When he looked over, he didn't see a thing. No movement. No sound. No smells.

Just him.

Just him and his thoughts all over again.

He listened to his racing heart. Looked down. The daisy he'd brought along with him was crushed. Crushed under the force of his fingers. All because of the memories.

The memories of what he'd done.

Of what he'd become.

"I'm sorry," he said, soon realising how ridiculous apologising to a headstone actually was.

He thought back. Thought back to Sarah. One of the last things she'd said to him.

"Go back to Riversford. Or keep on looking for some kind of safe haven. You do whatever you have to do. Just stay yourself. 'Cause yourself is fucking amazing, Hayden McCall."

Well, he had gone back to Riversford. One of the first journeys he'd made after leaving Sarah. He'd gone back and hadn't found a soul. No Martha. No nothing.

So he'd started surviving for himself. Started taking time on the road. Seeing sights. Looting. Taking food. Water. The lot.

Then... the boy happened.

He cast that thought aside once more. Remembered what Sarah said. About finding some kind of safe haven. To keep on being himself.

"I'm trying," Hayden said, fists tensed. "I'm—I'm really trying."

He heard voices over to the right.

Heard footsteps approaching.

He froze. Someone was here. Someone would find him. And he couldn't just walk away if they found him. He'd need to explain himself. He'd need to tell them who he was.

He'd have to get to know them.

But he couldn't.

He couldn't get to know anyone.

Because when he got to know people, bad things happened.

He crouched behind the headstone. Then, when he was sure the voices eased off, he moved to another headstone, moved between all of them until he reached the graveyard gates.

And then he saw torchlight shine right over him.

He stopped. Felt himself in the light, like an animal on a country lane staring at an approaching car.

"Do you see him?"

Those words.

Those fucking words.

He listened to the footsteps pick up. Heart racing. Mind spinning.

"Hey! You okay over there?"

He wanted to turn around. He wanted to respond. To tell them who he was. To learn about them. To speak with them about... about anything.

But then the memories of those he'd lost filled his mind.

Newbie.

Sarah.

The boy.

Clarice...

No, don't remember Clarice don't remember—

You stood by and watched them take her head off.

No!

You failed as a leader. You failed as a human being. You failed as a brother.

"Just... just wait there. Don't move. Don't... Hey!"

Hayden didn't stay put.

He couldn't stay put.

He climbed the fence. Disappeared into the trees. Behind him, he heard the approaching footsteps. The shouts. People like him. Desperate for company. Desperate for some kind of meaning in this world.

But they wouldn't get it.

Not from him.

Because he couldn't be around other people.

He couldn't lead other people.

People died when he made decisions.

So he ran into the night. Ran away from the churchyard. Ran away from Sarah's memorial.

He came to this town for a reason. A reason that he was still working up the courage to explore.

But now, he had no choice.

Now, he had to run.

Now, he had to find what he'd come here for.

CHAPTER FOUR

Hayden's mind swirled with all kinds of thoughts, all kinds of feelings, as he stood outside the semi-detached house on Westwood Lane.

The moonlight shone down brightly on the little side road in Hindley Green. The weather was cool, but all the running he'd done meant he didn't feel so bad. The street was quiet. No smell of death in the air. No sound of zombies groaning, staggering towards him.

Just this house.

This house he'd visited the town of Wigan for in the first place.

He walked up the driveway. Walked past the silver Toyota Celica. Dust covered it. Didn't look like it'd been touched in a long, long time.

Hayden wasn't sure whether that was a good or a bad thing anymore.

He walked up to the front door. Put a hand on the handle. No luck. Another search for a spare key on his hands.

He looked everywhere—under the plant pot, under the car, around the side of the house. No sign.

So Danny was just as much a security nut as he used to be.

Hayden walked around the back of the house. It'd been six years since he'd seen Danny. He called him "cousin," but that was more a token name cause they'd known each other since they were little kids. They always used to play out together when Hayden lived around Hindley. Always used to ride their bikes together. Smoked their first cigarettes together.

When Hayden moved away from Hindley, he kept up contact with Danny until they both turned about fifteen, sixteen. Not that Danny didn't *try* keeping in touch. Hayden's fault, really. All Hayden's fault. So many times he'd wanted to call his old mate. So many times he meant to Facebook message him. Just never got around to it. There was always another bill to pay, another mission on GTA to complete, another joint to smoke.

Then the world collapsed and everyone was gone.

The opportunity was gone.

Now was his chance.

He pulled himself over the wooden fence at the back of the house. Found himself glancing side to side, checking no one was looking. It didn't matter if anyone *was*, but a sense of lawfulness was inherent. Reactionary. Very hard to shake off.

Seeing nobody, Hayden dropped down into Danny's garden.

He looked around. Looked at the rope swing that snapped once when Bill Croft was playing with them. Not a big fall, but Bill cracked his head open. Wailed like a baby. Never lived that one down when they got back to school.

Hayden felt his body relaxing as the memories took over.

He wasn't sure how long he stood there before snapping out of the nostalgia, realising where he was, why he was here.

He turned to Danny's house. Looked at the glass doors of the conservatory. He knew Danny still lived here 'cause one of his final Facebook pictures tagged him in this garden.

Hayden walked across the grass. Walked over to the conservatory.

Danny was always so rational. Always so good at dealing with bad situations.

But a zombie apocalypse?

Would Danny be good enough to deal with that?

Hayden wasn't sure. He wasn't sure anyone was, really.

It was all just luck. It was all just a waiting game.

A pointless waiting game of playing leader until the pretend leader died and then someone else got to play leader... then they died too.

He stopped at the conservatory door.

A slight shiver covered him when he saw it was ajar.

He felt a quiver in his stomach. Saw silhouettes moving in the corners of his eyes. *No. They aren't there. All in your head. All in your imagination.*

He pushed the door open. Listened to it creak through the conservatory. He wasn't exactly sure why he'd come back to see his old friend. He didn't want to meet any new people. He didn't want to form any kind of bonds. And more than anything, he didn't want to lead. Because he couldn't lead. When he led, people died.

So many people, dead because of him.

Better to just float along. Take life one step at a time.

Alone.

But Danny felt different, for some reason. He was an old friend. Him and Hayden understood each other. Understood each other in ways the new world couldn't change.

Going back to Danny was like going back to his old life. A life free of responsibilities. A life where he didn't have to prove himself to anybody.

A life he could just enjoy—

He heard something rustling around in the lounge.

Nausea welled up inside Hayden. He closed the conservatory door, turned the lock. Walked over to the back of the conservatory, slowly. Squinted in the darkness. The moonlight shone in through the front window, but it didn't do much to help him. Just illuminated the dust floating around this room. Lit up the massive television perched on the wall. Revealed old computer magazines. Crime thrillers, like that bullshit McDone series Danny always went on about on social media. Films. Games.

All untouched.

Like it was some kind of showroom.

Like the world had just fallen to sleep.

Hayden walked into the lounge. Saw photographs of Danny perched on the mantlepiece. He still lived with his parents. Got a bit of stick for it, but he was a good lad from what Hayden knew. An ambitious lad doing everything he could to do freelance work on websites. He paid his rent. His parents supported him. He kept his head down and focused, just like he always had.

Now, Hayden just had to find him. So much to talk about. So much to catch up on. So much to—

He heard the rustling again. Only it wasn't coming from the lounge. It was coming from the hallway. From upstairs. A tapping. A tapping on the wall.

Hayden rubbed the back of his neck, then walked over to the hallway door.

The tapping continued as he approached. The only sounds he could hear were this tapping and the thudding of his heart. He lifted his hammer. Held it aloft. If Danny were out there—"out there" meaning zombified—Hayden would just have to deal with him. He'd have to detach himself. Just like he always had.

He wasn't sure how easy it would be. And that's what stopped him visiting Danny sooner. He'd worried. Worried about what kind of condition Danny might be in. Worried about what he'd think if Danny was gone.

In a way, he didn't want to find Danny here. Because not finding Danny here meant he'd got away.

Not finding Danny here kept his fate a mystery...

His thoughts stopped when he heard the buzzing at the top of the stairs.

When he saw the source of the tapping.

Danny hadn't got away. He was still in his house. Still in his boxer shorts, for that matter.

Only his jogging bottoms were wrapped around his neck.

He was hanging from the bannister.

Hayden's chest tightened. He wanted to run. Wanted to be alone. Wanted to get away. Wanted to go before the silhouettes came. Before the boy returned to his memories. Reminded him of what he'd done. Of what he'd—

Danny moved.

Hayden blinked. Looked up at Danny's hanging body. He'd seen him move. Definitely seen him move.

"Danny?"

He walked up the first step. Heart racing.

"Danny? Are..."

He saw the bite wound on Danny's arm. The chunk of flesh missing from his skin.

And then Danny lunged for him.

Hayden tumbled back. Fell off the bottom step, landed on the Welcome mat.

Danny struggled against his jogging bottoms. His eyes had popped out with the fall. His skin was completely purple.

The fall. The fall mustn't have broken his neck.

He'd been bitten so he'd hung himself.

And he hadn't finished the job effectively.

He looked at the blood drooling down Danny's mouth. Looked at his lips, which he'd bitten away to the point of mashing them up. And Hayden couldn't do anything but stare. Stare up at his friend. Danny. The last person on earth he could think of.

Gone.

Gone, just like everyone else.

All your fault. All your—

"No!"

His heart pounded in his ears. His vision tunnelled in on Danny.

He stormed up the stairs.

Saw all the dead. All the dead who'd killed those he loved. All the people who'd hurt him.

Saw all the loss he'd experienced, saw the voice inside his head right in front of him.

Tears rolling down his cheeks, he pulled back his hammer.

Smacked it into Danny's neck.

Hard.

Harder.

Harder.

He wasn't sure how long he beat his old friend to death. Blood crusted on his hands. His body twitched. He couldn't focus outside himself. Just on the memories.

Sarah.

The boy.

Clarice.

His parents.

And now Danny.

Everything he'd had. Everything he'd taken so for granted.

Everything he'd lost.

He hobbled away from Danny's limply hanging body. Walked into his lounge. Climbed on the white leather sofa, curled up into the foetal position.

There was no world for him anymore. Because he wasn't strong enough.

He couldn't save people.

He squeezed his eyes shut. Saw the image of the boy in his mind. The boy he'd left behind. The boy he hadn't had the balls to run back and save.

The boy he'd watched die.

He squeezed them tighter as images of his parents, of Clarice, of Newbie and Sarah and Danny and everyone, replayed through his mind on a loop.

His older sister Annabelle, hanging, all those years ago.

People die because of you.

He felt tears dampening his cheeks. Felt his eyes straining as he tensed his eyelids even more.

There was nothing for him anymore.

No place for him anymore.

So he curled up tighter.

Waited for the inevitable moment.

The only ending in all this hopelessness.

Waited to die.

CHAPTER FIVE

"Help me! Please!"

The voice.

The voice of a young boy.

Or was it a girl?

Was it his...

Sister.

Clarice.

No, his older sister, Annabelle.

She was upset.

She was crying about something.

She was—

Hayden was in a corridor. In a darkened corridor. Rain lashed down outside. The moon kept on drifting across the frosted window, moving from side to side, bathing Hayden in light. The scream echoed around his mind.

"Please! Please don't leave!"

He couldn't leave. No. He had to do the right thing. He had to save the boy.

He had to save everyone.

He tried to run. But his feet were stuck. Glued down by something.

Blood.

No...

He looked down and saw the faces of those he cared for. Clarice. Sarah. Danny. Annabelle. Mum. Dad. Everyone.

He saw their greying faces staring up at him with angry eyes.

Saw their mouths wrapping around his feet.

Holding him down.

Trying to bite.

He heard the scream again. Heard the cry.

When he looked up, he saw the boy.

He was at the other side of the window. Outside the house. Banging against the glass. Young. Six, seven, maybe older, maybe younger. Wasn't sure. Couldn't be sure.

All that mattered was he was in danger. He was screaming. He needed help.

Hayden tried to shout at the boy. Tried to tell him everything was going to be okay. That he'd be there for him any moment.

But he couldn't open his mouth. His mouth was glued shut.

He couldn't run.

He couldn't cry.

The boy's screams got louder and louder, the bright light of the moon drifting behind him once more...

He looked into the eyes of the boy and he saw it now. Saw it like he always did. Like he always saw it.

"You take a look around the back and I'll..."

Blood drooling out of the boy's eyes.

"DON'T LEAVE ME!"

Fear filling the boy's pale face.

"...Should be a way in round there."

Hayden pushed harder. Pushed to run. But he knew it was pointless. Knew it was no good. He was trapped. Held down by the people he cared about. The people he'd lost.

All because he wasn't strong enough for this world.

And now he had to watch.

He saw the teeth around the little boy's neck.

Saw it, just like he'd seen it three weeks ago.

He heard the final, deafening shriek from the boy.

And then he watched the boy's neck explode.

Watched blood splatter all over the window.

Watched it smash the glass—

Hayden jolted upright. Heart racing. Sweat covering his forehead. He looked around, struggling for breath. He was in Danny's house. On Danny's sofa. Must've fallen asleep. Must've...

He saw the light drift through the conservatory, into the lounge.

His body froze.

People.

He rolled over the back of the sofa. Crouched behind it. Didn't know what to do. Didn't know where to go. Only they couldn't see him. He couldn't let anyone see him.

Even if they weren't bad people, he couldn't run the risk of them seeing him.

Because he needed to be alone.

"Jelly. Peanut butter. Jesus, there's a whole bunch of treats in here."

"Keep your voice down, prick. It's not your fucking fat fetish we're here to please."

Hayden saw the light hit the top of the sofa. A torchlight. Just as bright as the moon in his dream. Thinking of it, he'd heard voices. Muffled voices from outside his nightmare.

If only he'd woken up sooner.

If only he'd...

Someone stepped into the lounge.

Hayden crouched further. Held his breath. Listened to the heavy footsteps move across the wooden flooring. He could smell aftershave on the people. Decent aftershave. Probably something they'd stolen. No, *definitely* something they'd stolen.

The men who valued appearance in spite of all the destruction were definitely ones to avoid in this world.

"You take a look upstairs. I'll scan the lounge."

The other man sighed.

"What was that?"

"What was what?"

"That fucking sigh. What's that about?"

Silence from the other guy. Then, "I—I just think we've got plenty already. Gonna be one cramped truck if we wedge any more in."

"And you think that's a problem?"

"I just think—"

"Ssh. I think I heard something."

Hayden's body tensed. He looked around for his hammer but...

"A hammer?"

His stomach sank. His hammer. He'd left his fucking hammer lying on the sofa.

Covered in blood.

Danny's blood.

He heard the man's footsteps get closer to the sofa. Heard one of the men reach right down towards it. The torchlight was so close. So close to revealing Hayden's location. To revealing where he was.

He waited for them to move the light behind the sofa. For them to investigate.

"Might come in handy," the aggressive guy with the deeper voice said.

They stepped away from the sofa. And Hayden heard their footsteps moving towards the hallway door.

"Guess we'll both check upstairs seeing as you're too pussy to go up yourself."

"I'm not too pussy. I'm just... ah, shit."

Hayden lifted his neck slightly. He knew from the cursing that they'd just found Danny's hanging body.

"He definitely dead?"

"See the shape of his fucking head? Looks pretty worse for wear to me."

Hayden listened to their footsteps climb the creaky stairs. As they climbed, he crept over the back of the sofa. Did all he could not to make any noise as he stood there in the darkness. He looked outside. Saw more movement. Heard some kind of engine rumbling. A truck? And what was that they said about stuffing something inside?

He wasn't keen on sticking around to find out.

He crept across the floorboards. Reached the conservatory door. They'd smashed the glass completely. His route out into the garden lay ahead.

Just had to climb the fence.

Then run.

Run to...

Well. He didn't know anymore. Just away from here. Away from people. Away from everything.

Find a quiet place to roll over and die.

A place in the bushes to rot in peace.

He crept across the conservatory floor, the muffled voices of the two men receding further up the stairs. He climbed over the cracked glass, being careful not to nip his feet and stepped out into the fresh night air. Chilly. Way too chilly. Felt even worse that he'd been suddenly jolted from his sleep.

His mind still wasn't tuned in.

Wasn't thinking clearly.

He ran across the grass. The sound of the engine seemed louder now he was outside. He didn't even want to look at the vehicle. Didn't even want to acknowledge it was there.

Just like the silhouettes drifting into his consciousness.

Just like the memories of the boy...

He reached for the top of the fence. Pulled himself up. Just drop onto the other side. Run away. Simple as that. Simple as—

"Hey!"

He heard the voice behind him.

And then he felt the light surround him.

He turned around. Looked up.

The two men were standing at Danny's bedroom window. Shining the light at Hayden.

"Don't move another muscle," the gruff-voiced guy said.

It was then that Hayden saw his gun.

Pointing right at him.

Finger on the trigger.

CHAPTER SIX

"Don't move another muscle, mate. This doesn't have to get messy."

Hayden gripped onto the top of the fence. His fingers ached. Shit—his entire body ached. He knew the street was on the other side. He knew he was just inches away from being surrounded by darkness, a nice change to the spotlight beaming down on him right now. He could hear the engine of the truck rumbling at the front of Danny's house. Swore he could hear more voices, too.

"Clive, I don't think we should—"

"Shut the fuck up," the gruff-voiced man—Clive—muttered. "Lower yourself from the fence and walk this way. It's important. Really. You're gonna wanna hear what we've got on offer."

Hayden smelled the fumes from the engine of the vehicle. That's where Clive was wrong. He didn't want to know what was in the truck. He didn't want any idea what these two were up to. What they were trying to "cramp" onto the truck. He didn't like the sound of it one bit.

So he kept hold of the fence.

Waited.

Wasn't sure what for exactly. Just something. A moment.

A moment of action.

"Let me tell you how this is gonna work. You're gonna climb down off that fence. Then we're gonna talk about the next step."

"Just tell him about the—"

"Fuck off!" Clive shouted at his companion. Hayden wasn't sure what they were hiding, but they were hiding something. Clive's friend knew something. He was trying to bargain with Hayden in some way. That much was obvious.

But Clive preferred the tough guy tactics.

"What's it gonna be?" Clive asked.

Hayden kept hold of the fence top.

Saw the torchlight readjust, making sure to keep him front and centre in their vision.

Hayden swallowed a lump in his throat.

Closed his eyes.

Took a deep breath.

And then he dragged himself up the side of the fence and threw himself over.

He waited for the bullets to pierce his body. Waited for them to split through his skin. To crack his bones.

But they didn't.

He hit the grassy verge on the other side of the fence. At the window, he heard Clive and his friend's commotion. Heard the shouts. The panic.

He heard them running away from the window. Down the stairs.

But he was out.

He was alive.

Clive hadn't fired his gun.

Hayden couldn't deny his curiosity. Why hadn't he shot him? Why hadn't he just finished him off?

What did he want him for?

His thoughts were interrupted when he saw two figures wander out of the detached house across the road.

He didn't need a light to know they were zombies.

He instinctively went to lift his hammer. Realised he didn't have it anymore. Shit. Stupid idea leaving it on the sofa. Almost got him ratted out, now probably end up getting him killed.

"Wait!"

The shouting echoed from Danny's house. Footsteps getting closer to the conservatory.

The engine of the truck around the front rumbling.

Hayden looked at the road ahead. A dead end. A cul de sac. But he knew if he managed to climb the fence at the end of the street, he'd find himself in his old school fields. Long grass. Vast. Lot of area without any kind of shelter.

But better than being here.

Better than risking staying put.

So he sprinted.

He sprinted down the road, away from the zombies and the men. He saw lights shine across the street. Saw them scan around. Did all he could to dodge them, like he was Sam Fisher on *Splinter Cell* or something.

He saw the green metal fence in the distance. A bit more overgrown behind it than it used to be, but it was something. He could climb it. Land on the other side.

Run for his life.

He saw more movement in the houses to his left. He wondered if they were just figments of his imagination; mirages of his mind.

But then he heard their gasps and he knew he was out of luck.

Zombies.

More zombies.

He needed to get to that fence. Get over it. Get away.

He saw the end of the road approaching. Saw the kerb he once sprained his ankle on, kicking it during a football game. The other kids laughed. Danny laughed.

After seeing Danny strung up in his house, eyes bulging, skin as pale as a dead fish, it was hard to imagine he'd ever laughed in his entire life.

No.

No time to reminisce.

No time to wish things were different.

Just had to get away.

He reached the kerb when the lights surrounded him. He heard voices. Muffled voices shouting at one another. *"It's him! Stop him!"*

He didn't know who these people were. Just that they'd broken into Danny's. They were looking for something.

And now they were chasing him.

He heard the bullets pepper around him. Heard them skim across the concrete as he reached the metal fence. He waited for one of them to pierce his flesh. To knock him down.

But again, none of them were hitting him.

As if they were trying *not* to hit him.

Why would they try not to hit him?

Why did they want him?

His mind was racing so much that he didn't see the zombie on the other side of the fence.

But it saw him.

It grabbed his chest. Dragged Hayden towards the fence. Good job it had a fat face because its mouth was right between the metal poles, snapping away, inches from Hayden's skin.

Hayden punched its hand. Tried to pull back, to drag himself free. He looked over his shoulder. Saw more of the figures—the dead figures—closing in. Further behind, the group. Five of them. All of them armed. All of them with torches.

Even further back, he saw the truck they'd spoken of.

A black truck with a compartment on the back.

A compartment to put... whatever they put in there.

He didn't want to find out.

He couldn't find out.

He grabbed the side of the fence. Pulled himself up. As he did, the zombie didn't let go of his black bomber jacket. It just clung on by the tips of its fingers, still snapping away.

The dead weight was nigh on impossible to lift. But Hayden kept on pulling. Kept on lifting, straining, until he reached the top of the fence. Until the zombie's neck was level with the sharp spike at the top of the metal.

Then, when he was absolutely sure the zombie's chin was in place, he let go of the fence.

He fell to the ground. And for a terrifying moment, he thought the zombie might just fall with him.

It clutched onto him at first.

And then the pole split through its chin, pierced its head.

Hayden looked up at the zombie. It kept on snapping away, dangling onto the sharp metal by its head. He hadn't quite got its neck. But he didn't need to. It wasn't a threat. Not anymore. Pity for it. Damned pity. But he didn't have time to sympathise.

He rolled over. A sharp pain split through his right shoulder. Shit. Must've dislocated it or something. Not good. Not good at all.

He dragged himself up. Stretched for the top of the fence.

The pain in his right shoulder intensified.

"Shit."

He took a few deep, steadying breaths. His mind spun. He had to climb the fence. He had to fight through the pain and he had to make it. There was no negotiating. The footsteps were approaching. Time was running out. Soon, they'd capture him. Soon, he'd be dead.

Or at least his solitude would.

And that wasn't a good thing.

He went to reach for the fence again when he heard something directly behind.

An engine. An engine getting closer.

Gunfire popping.

A door opening.

Then closing.

Boots hitting the ground.

"No need to run anymore, my friend," a voice said.

Hayden stared at the green metal fence. The pain in his shoulder grew more and more intense. He couldn't get away. He couldn't climb. He was trapped. This was it.

He turned around. Looked into the bright lights shining on him.

A man stepped forward. A man with shoulder length black hair, with thick glasses. He was dressed in a leather jacket and skinny blue jeans. But it didn't look right. Looked like he was playing a role. Looked more like a doctor or a vet than a thug. No stereotypes intended.

"Just let me go," Hayden winced, the pain in his shoulder creeping up.

The man smiled. He lowered his gun first, then his torch. "Oh, we will. We will. In fact, that's exactly what we're gonna do."

Hayden frowned. "What do you—"

"Steven, turn her around. About time we showed the gentleman his ride."

The truck turned around. The man walked up to the door. Grabbed a handle.

"My ride?"

He turned back to Hayden. Smiled again. "Congratulations, bossman. You've won a front row ticket to eternal safety."

He lowered the handle.

Pulled open the door.

It took Hayden a few seconds to realise what he was looking at.

But when he realised, every muscle in his body tensed.

CHAPTER SEVEN

Hayden couldn't find the words to respond to the scene in front of him.

"Well? You getting on board or am I gonna have to throw you on?"

The long-haired man with glasses smiled, but as Hayden stood there in the darkness, the moon now hiding behind thick clouds, he sensed an air of sincerity to his words.

Because the truck in front of him was filled with people.

Literally stuffed to the brim with people. All of them clinging on to whatever they could. They stared out at Hayden with wide, tired eyes. Somewhere near the back of the crowd, a baby cried. Flies buzzed around them, their skin covered in a film of dirt. He could smell the sweat and the piss from out here.

But there were people.

And they weren't trying to flee the truck.

That had to mean something.

"Respect for running off from us," the long-haired man said, walking towards Hayden. "I'll give you that. Thing is we're new to this. New employees, if you will. And different members of the team have different methods. So Clive's sorry for scarin' you off. Ain't that right, Clive?"

Hayden looked at Clive, the bulky man with the gruff voice who'd chased him from Danny's house. Clive grunted. Offered the smallest, slightest nod imaginable. Didn't look like he was all that apologetic.

The long-haired man stopped in front of Hayden. Lights shone on the pair of them from behind. The mass of people looked out, not speaking, not saying a word. Didn't feel right for some reason. Felt surreal. More people than he'd seen in one location since... since... he didn't even know when.

"Sorry. I should introduce myself. The name's Thomas. Thomas Morgan."

He held out a hand.

Hayden just stared at it.

Thomas nodded. Sniffed. Pulled his hand away. "I get you're scared. Get this ain't how you saw your night goin' down. But we're here to help you. Just like we're helpin' all these other people."

"My hammer."

Thomas frowned. "Your... I don't think you understand—"

"My hammer," Hayden said, glaring at Clive. "I want my hammer. Then I want to leave."

Clive glanced at Thomas, Thomas back at Clive. Thomas started laughing. Scratched the back of his head. "I don't think you're gettin' me properly. We're giving you an opportunity. A chance to join us. Someplace safe down south. Don't need to worry about a hammer. None of these need to worry about—"

"I heard you," Hayden said, trying to keep his composure. "And I heard what you're offering. But I want my hammer. I want to leave."

Thomas laughed again, but this time it was more of a snort of bafflement. "You—you're sayin' you don't want to join us?"

Hayden looked past Thomas. Looked at the bloodshot eyes of

the people in the truck. Men. Women. Children. All ages. All races. All of them staying put.

In front of them, these people dressed in the strangest assortment of clothes, all shining lights on him.

Armed.

"This safe place. What kind of safe place is it?"

"The kind that keeps you safe," Thomas said, chuckling.

"Nowhere's safe."

"And I can see why you might believe that. All I can say is... well, our place is different."

"Different, how?"

Thomas smiled. "That's summat you're gonna have to see for yourself. But you will approve when you see it. I can assure you of that."

Hayden stared into Thomas' eyes. He wasn't sure how sincere he was being. Very few sincere people left in this world. But even if he was... what good was another safe place? What good was another false beacon of hope?

Better to just accept their fate. To walk alone.

Because with safe places came leadership, and with leadership came collapse.

Always.

Hayden cleared his throat. Butterflies fluttered in his chest. Not used to addressing other people. Wasn't the best communicator before the world collapsed, let alone now. But he had to try. He had to show his manners. "I appreciate your offer," he said, smiling. He'd read in some book that smiling made a more positive impression than anything else. He'd read a lot of books in the last few months. "But right now I don't think I'm ready for what you're advertising."

A look of disappointment on Thomas' face. A few sighs and grumbles from his companions.

"So I'd—I'd appreciate it if you gave me back my weapon and let me leave."

"Leave where?" Thomas asked.

"That's..." He was about to say it was none of Thomas' fucking business. But he remembered his manners at the last second. Smiled again. "I have a place. Just a small place. I... I have someone I'm looking after there. I can't just leave them."

"Then take us to them. They're more than welcome on the merry bus!"

"Respectfully... no," Hayden said. There. He'd said it. Got it off his chest. "I'm sorry. Grateful for your offer. Really am. But it's not for me. Not now."

There was silence amongst the group. A taste of sweat in the air from the mass of people in the back of the truck. He couldn't go in there. Not with all those people. He couldn't go from the life he'd been living to *that* all of a sudden.

But Thomas wasn't saying anything in return.

No one was saying anything in return.

Eventually, Thomas sighed. He nodded. "Close the doors."

Clive walked to the back of the truck. Closed the doors.

The people disappeared, as too did Hayden's chance.

"Give the man his hammer."

Clive tutted. "But—"

"Just give it him. Respect his wishes."

Clive shook his head. Then he reached into his pocket, walked over to Hayden and handed him his hammer.

Adrenaline made Hayden's muscles shake. He gripped onto the hammer. He was okay. He was going to be okay. These people weren't bad. They were letting him go.

But if they weren't bad... maybe he should be joining them?

No. Stupid thought. Idealistic thought.

"I really wish you'd agreed to join us," Thomas said, walking closer to Hayden. He shook his head slowly, his expression stony.

"I—I hope everything goes well. At your safe place."

Thomas stopped. Held out that hand again. "Me too. Me too."

Hayden put the hammer into his left hand.

Reached out to shake Thomas'.

He saw Thomas swing the taser at him with his other hand. Saw it and knew what was happening, right away.

But he was already too late.

Thomas pressed the taser into Hayden's left arm.

Burning, crackling sensations stormed through Hayden's body, made every muscle tense and twitch violently.

The hammer fell on the road.

"I really wish you'd just said yes," Thomas said, as Hayden fell to the ground, trying to move, desperate to shake free.

Two men grabbed hold of him. Dragged him to his feet. Pulled him towards the truck.

Hayden started to scream. Felt a hand cover his mouth right away.

"You don't say a word about this," Thomas said, sweat rolling down his forehead. "You don't say a word to anyone. Or you'll all die. The men. The women. The children. You'll all die. And you'll be solely responsible."

Hayden struggled. Struggled as they pushed him towards the back of the truck. Towards the darkness.

"So," Thomas said, putting a hand on the truck door. "You ready to take a trip?"

CHAPTER EIGHT

The journey in the truck was even worse than Hayden could ever have imagined.

He couldn't see a thing in the dark, windowless rear compartment. Nothing but the backs of heads. The mass of people. There were so many stuffed in like sardines that it was crushing, borderline impossible to breathe. Didn't help that the truck kept driving over bumps, knocking elbows into faces, starting confrontations and arguments. Also didn't help that it reeked in here. Reeked of sweat, piss, shit. *Also* didn't help that a baby just kept on wailing somewhere near the back of the truck.

Simply put, this place was hell.

Hayden's mouth was dry. He couldn't remember the last time he'd had a drink. Didn't know how long he'd even been travelling, just that it had to be morning now. The darkness in this truck was suffocating. Disorienting. He knew the truth—he could be anywhere.

He wanted to talk. Talk about where they were heading. Where they were going.

But the pain in his left arm reminded him of the taser. The bolts of electricity that tore through his body.

Thomas' promise.

"You don't say a word to anyone. Or you'll all die. The men. The women. The children. You'll all die. And you'll be solely responsible."

He didn't know these people. But he didn't want to take a chance. He didn't want to be responsible for any more death.

He couldn't live with it.

The truck stopped a few times on the way. Conversation picked up amongst the group. People gathered around the back door, excitement building in the air. But every time the truck stopped, it always started up again, accompanied by the slam of a door, the chatter of the guards.

Because that's what they felt like. Guards.

This was a kind of prison.

The truck picked a few more people up on the way, too. Most complied. Most were thankful. All of them added to the mass crush.

But occasionally, someone turned down Thomas' offer. Occasionally, they'd refuse. Walk away.

The doors would close.

Just like they had for Hayden.

And then that same person would willingly walk inside just moments later, clutching their arms.

Hayden wondered how many other people had turned down the first offer. How many more in here had been tasered into joining Thomas' group.

He wanted to know. But he didn't want to risk finding out.

He knew the lives of the people in here depended on his silence.

After what had to be another two hours, the truck pulled up again. Only this time, something different happened.

The engine stopped.

Sensing the change, more people pushed up against the doors. Someone stamped on Hayden's right ankle, nudged into his dodgy shoulder and made him wince.

He looked at the door. Losing breath as the crush grew stronger. Tension building up inside, manifesting within.

He was going to suffocate.

He was going to die in here.

He was going to be crushed.

He was—

The doors of the truck opened up.

Light filled the back of the truck. Bright morning sun, disorienting, migraine-inducing.

"Single file," one of the guards called, lowering a ramp. "Hey, hey! Single file."

As the group in the back of the truck climbed out of the vehicle, another of the guards handed out bottles of water. The people were so thankful, so grateful, taking bottles and sharing the water between their families.

Hayden allowed himself to fall to the back of the queue. He wanted a chance to properly analyse his surroundings while he had an opportunity. Figure out where he was. Where Thomas' group had taken him, taken all these people.

He wanted to see this "safe haven" for what it really was.

But as he walked out, he didn't see anything significant. Not a town, like he expected. Not even a bunch of tents, flimsy enough for the zombies to rip through.

He just saw a sprawling brick building.

Each and every one of the truck travellers being led in through a double door by more smiley people, these dressed in black.

"Hey. Take your water."

Hayden turned to his side. Saw Clive glaring at him. "I'm okay. Thanks—"

"Not an option," Clive said. He stuffed the water bottle into Hayden's chest.

Hayden took hold of it reluctantly. Inspected the cap. Sealed. A good sign. He'd seen how easy it was to poison water after what happened with Holly and Sarah. He wondered where Holly was. Whether she and her husband were still in Holyhead. Whether they were happy. Whether they were safe.

Then he heard a bell ring from the wall above.

"Ah fuck," Clive said, jogging away from Hayden. He lifted a walkie talkie, spoke into it. "Got a breach. Three guards down to the west fences asap. Over."

Hayden watched Clive run away, gun in hand. He saw walls, then. Huge brick walls with barbed wire wrapped around the top. Ladders propped up against them, one of them which Clive climbed, three people joining him in an instant.

"Keep moving," someone muttered.

Hayden saw Thomas on his right. He was smiling again. But he could see right through that smile now. See it for what it was. A fallacy.

"What is this place?" Hayden asked, as he walked towards the entrance.

Thomas smiled. "Like I said. It's someplace safe. Now, please. Keep moving. We've got a lot of allocating to do today."

Before Hayden could query Thomas about what he meant by "allocating," Thomas disappeared through the door. Hayden was stopped by a small woman of Chinese descent at the doorway. She was holding a clip pad with a thick pile of papers attached to it.

"Name," she said.

"Um, it's Hayden. Hayden Mc..." He thought about giving his own name. Something told him to hold off the full truth. "Hayden McDone."

The woman jotted down his name. Pulled a red sticker from the side of her pad. Pressed it onto his chest.

She looked him in the eyes and smiled. "Welcome to Salvation."

He didn't have any time to query the Chinese woman. He heard gunfire peppering over the side of the walls, a few whoops and cheers from the guards.

And then he was inside.

He was soon ushered into a line by more armed guards. He realised he was in some kind of reception area. White tiles. Grey walls. All very lifeless. But the walls outside. They were big. And it seemed like they had everyone well drilled around here.

Hell, maybe this place *could* be safe.

When he reached the back of the reception area, he saw three doors. People were organised by their stickers into groups. Some of the stickers were removed, replaced with other colours. The people running Salvation—Thomas' people—barely looked the new arrivals in the eyes. Like they were just cattle.

The comparison unsettled Hayden. He hoped he was off the mark.

"Okay." A man with long strands of hair despite the balding on his scalp walked in front of Hayden, in front of his line. "We're going to give you all a number as you pass. You remember that number. It's the most important number in your life right now. Understand?"

A few grunts. A few nods of approval.

"Okay. If you'll all just step forward, that'd be—"

The man's voice was interrupted by a scream. Someone over on the right. They were halfway through the door. Trying to get out. Trying to get away.

Guards were pinning the woman down. Telling her everything was okay. That they were here to help.

Hayden sensed the mood inside the building changing with every scream from the woman. His heart pounded. What had she seen? Why was she was so afraid? And why was he willingly walking towards it if he was—

"Number seven."

Hayden felt the marker pen on his left hand.

He saw the number seven being drawn onto it.

Then, out of nowhere, a stamp pressed into the middle of his left arm, like the needles of a TB jab.

The balding man half-smiled as the screaming woman was dragged away. "Tetanus shot. You'll need it in here. And don't worry about her, pal. She doesn't know what's good for her."

Hayden squeezed his burning arm, barely processing unfolding events. "What is this pl–"

He didn't finish his question.

The balding man pushed him through the door.

And all of a sudden he was in the clutches of two people. Two armed guards. Both dragging him along. Emptying his pockets while they walked.

It was then that Hayden realised what this place was. Where he was.

He tried to struggle. Tried to break free.

As he saw the metal bars.

As he saw the locked cells.

The people trapped behind them.

This wasn't *like* a prison.

It *was* a prison.

The guards dragged him to an open door. Pushed him inside it.

"Wait," Hayden shouted.

He threw himself towards the cell door. But it slammed shut. Slammed shut before he could do anything about it.

The guard locked the door. Smiled at Hayden as he kicked out, struggled to break free. "Don't fret, number seven. This is your new home. Your new safe place."

"It's a prison! It's a fucking prison!"

The guard just kept on smiling as he walked away. "Enjoy your first day, number seven. Settle down. Then we'll be back for induction tomorrow morning. Or tomorrow evening, depending on your behaviour."

As the guards walked away, Hayden grabbed the metal bars of the cell and screamed. Rattled them, no regard for his pained shoulder, no regard for his sanity, or for anything.

He was stuck.

He was trapped.

He'd walked right into a trap, and he'd allowed himself to.

Idiot.

Fucking idiot.

This was why he couldn't lead.

This was why he couldn't even trust himself.

This was—

"If you want to get out of this place outside a body bag, you might want to quit your screaming right this second."

CHAPTER NINE

Hayden turned around and looked at the back of his cell.

He'd heard a voice. Somewhere behind him, away from all the madness of the prison, he'd heard someone. So clearly that it sounded like they were in the cell with him.

But nobody was there.

Just a low bed. A thin mattress laid on top of it. A toilet. A sink. Wasn't sure if there was any flowing water supply in here. Probably not. Probably why they'd given him the drinking bottle.

But the voice.

Was it real?

Or just another figment of his imagination?

Was it—

"I'm in the cell next to you. Come close to the wall and we can talk."

The hairs on Hayden's arms raised. He wasn't imagining things. He wasn't going fucking crazy.

There really was somebody talking to him.

A woman.

A woman in the cell next door.

He staggered over to the left of his cell. Crouched down. Put his ear to where he thought the voice came from.

"Don't make it look obvious," the woman said. "Just lean back. You'll hear me and I'll hear you."

Hayden leaned against the wall. He wasn't sure how this woman knew he'd been "making it look obvious" in the first place. But she was right. Maybe people before him had made the same mistake.

Or maybe she could see, somehow.

"Who... who are you?" he asked.

"Name's Miriam."

"Miriam. I'm Hayden—"

"That's not important right now. What's important is your decision."

"My decision?"

"About whether you want to stay locked up in this 'camp' forever. Safe for a while, possibly. But locked up. Like a prisoner."

Hayden looked over at the cell door. Saw more doors like his on the other side of the prison. "Don't think we have much choice."

"Not right now. But strange things can happen if you're willing to fight for them."

Hayden rubbed the bridge of his nose. His head was banging. He wanted nothing more than sleep. "Look. I... I was bundled in a truck back in Wigan. I've spent the whole night travelling down to... to wherever this is, being crushed by masses of people. Oh, and I was tasered. Tasered to get me into the truck."

"Then their methods are getting more violent," Miriam said.

"Whose methods? Who are these people?"

Silence from Miriam.

"Miriam, who are—"

"Don't know who exactly. But I know where we are. We're in

the Midlands. Just south of Crewe. And I know what these people know about."

"You aren't making any sense."

"There's a wall. Towards the south of England. A wall splitting the country into north and south."

Hayden frowned. He looked over at the door of the cell. Looked out at the people lying on their beds. Crying. Caged in. "What wall?"

"Apparently they built this wall pretty rapidly when Britain started falling. A fence system. A way to keep the zombies out. A north-south divide. A real safe place. A place of refuge."

Hayden couldn't help but shake his head. "Sounds like a fantasy."

"You sound like a cynic."

"Isn't everyone nowadays?"

"No," Miriam said, pausing between her words. "The best thing to be is a realist. Then a fantasist. Then a cynic."

"And why's that?"

"At least the fantasist still has something to look forward to. The cynic might as well be dead."

Hayden pondered Miriam's words. Truth be told, none of them seemed to make sense. Something about a wall. A wall dividing Britain in two. "Who... who made this wall?"

"What's left of the government, I guess. Maybe the armed forces. A place to take people. To start again. Somewhere free of undead. No point clearing out the hundreds of thousands of dead above the wall. Might as well just leave them to fall themselves."

"And you believe this, why?"

A pause from Miriam.

The sound of footsteps clanging against the metal prison walkway.

"Miriam?"

"Because I reached it."

"You reached it?"

"I got to it. With my old group. We heard a rumour or two. Didn't have much hope left. And word's travelling anyway. Amazed you've not already heard of it."

"I... I don't mix with people much these days."

"That'd explain it."

Hayden had so many questions but none of them added up, made sense. "If you reached it then..."

"Why am I in here? Good question. Making my way towards it when this group scoots down from nowhere. Bundles me and my friends in the back of a truck with a bunch of children, old folks. Say they're taking us to a safe place. Now we're sceptical. Course we are. Start to worry when we spend hours on the journey. But it's already too late. In here before we know it. And not a thing we can do about it. Until now."

Miriam's answers didn't seem to be getting any less confusing. "Then who are these people?"

"My guess is a rival group. Some other power-hungry do-gooder who wants to keep things the way they are on the outside. Get the credit for restarting society from within, some bullshit like that. Dunno though. What's important is whether you're with us."

Hayden thought about Miriam's offer. "With you on what?"

"In ten seconds, I'm going to throw a sharp piece of wall tile out of the front of my cell. You're going to choose whether to take that tile or not. In an hour, or a few hours, you're going to get a visit from a guard called Tim. He'll be here to take you down to induction. You go with him. You've no choice there. When you reach the corridor with the old offices on the left, you have a choice."

"What choice?"

"Simple. You walk on with Tim and you continue your little prison life in here. Or you stab him in the neck."

"Stab him in the—?"

"You stab him. You take his keys. And his clothes if you have the time. And then you come back to my cell and you let me out. I'll take lead from there."

Hayden's heart raced. He didn't know what to say. "But—but what if—"

"I'm throwing the tile now."

"Miriam, I—"

The tile landed right in front of Hayden's cell. Right between the metal bars. Just in reach.

"Take it or leave it. Just know that by leaving it, you're condemning everyone in this place—yourself included—to a life in prison."

Hayden stared at the tile. At its sharp edge.

"Why can't you?" he asked.

"Why can't I what?"

"Why can't you stab the guard?"

"Because Tim isn't coming for me," Miriam said. "Not anymore. I get meals delivered. I get the occasional medical check. But I don't leave this cell, Hayden. And neither will you. That's why it needs to be you. You're my first neighbour since I got to this place. Please. Don't let this pass."

Hayden's mind raced. "But downstairs. The canteen."

"It's for show," Miriam said. "You really think they'd just let people wander 'round freely? Don't believe what they tell you. Don't believe their smiles. Don't even believe a fellow prisoner. 'Cause you don't know what the guards have told them."

Hayden's stomach tensed. "Then how do I trust you?"

Miriam chuckled. "That's your decision to make. Choose it wisely. Hold up. I think... shit."

"Miriam? What's up? What's wrong?"

"Shit. He's too early. Way too fucking early."

"What you talking about?"

"Tim," Miriam called. "He's... he's on his way down the corridor. To your cell. Right this fucking minute."

Hayden listened to the approaching footsteps of the guard called Tim.

The sharp-edged tile stared back at him from outside the bars.

CHAPTER TEN

Hayden listened to Tim's footsteps follow closely behind him.

He walked down the metal pathway in front of the cells. He looked inside those cells. Saw so many different faces. People staring back at him. And regardless of the smiley faces and positive quotes etched on the white walls of this building, they didn't look happy. They didn't look content.

Even the people who were smiling looked like they had a gun to their head.

Hayden remembered what Miriam told him.

"Don't believe their smiles."

Maybe they did have a gun to their head after all, of a sort.

"Come on, pal," Tim said, his voice friendly, jovial. "I'm not the quickest of walkers but dammit, you don't half drag your feet!"

Hayden glanced around. Looked at Tim. He was pretty old. Short, thinning grey hair. Round glasses so strong they magnified his eyes. Breath smelled of pickled onion.

But he seemed... nice. Friendly. He seemed okay.

"Don't believe their smiles."

Maybe what Miriam told him was true. Maybe he should be wary. Of other people. Of everyone in this place.

But how did that exclude her?

Who was to say she wasn't just setting Hayden up for some personal benefit of her own?

Shit, he hadn't even looked the woman in the eye yet. He'd just heard her voice. Heard her voice behind the cell wall. Heard some bullshit about a fence splitting the north and the south. About an old group of hers reaching it, then being tossed into the back of a truck—just like Hayden—and brought here.

As Hayden turned, climbed down the metal steps, every footstep echoing through the prison, he wondered if perhaps Miriam was lying. Maybe this was all some kind of test. A loyalty test. Maybe Tim was being nice for a reason—to lull him into a false sense of security.

Maybe he was just waiting for Hayden to attack. To take his opportunity. A way of sifting the loyal from the opportunists.

Or maybe he was just a guard called Tim.

Maybe there was a corridor coming up. A corridor with an old office on the left.

Maybe Miriam genuinely wanted Hayden to help her so they could get out of here.

It seemed outlandish. It seemed fucking mental.

But Hayden wasn't sure what to believe.

"Right-o, you," Tim said as the pair of them reached the bottom of the stairs. "This place is gonna be your second home for a while. Get to know it." He pointed at the canteen area. Pointed at the metal tables. People sat around them, eating, smiling and laughing together. They didn't look at Hayden. And Hayden wasn't sure why that was. Were they really engrossed in conversation? Or were they just actors playing a part? Building the false sense of security?

If so, why?

"Tell you what," Tim said, patting Hayden on his right shoulder.

Hayden winced.

"Ohh. I am sorry, fella. Hurt your shoulder?"

Hayden shook his head. "Just a bruise."

"We can get it checked out in med bay after your induction if it's really botherin' you. Might as well. Never saw the point of suffering in silence, y'know?"

"I'm fine. Honestly." Hayden forced a smile. He hoped it didn't come across as unnatural as it felt.

Big Tim chuckled. Tilted his head at the door in front. "Induction's through there. Shouldn't take too long. Just wanna get to know you. Learn what makes you tick. And vice versa. That okay with you?"

Hayden stopped at the door. The sound of chatter surrounded him, clouded his thoughts. The smells from the canteen seemed unnatural. He felt like he was dreaming. Like this was some sort of bullshit dream.

Maybe walking on would be the best option. Maybe living in a place like this wasn't so bad after all.

Locked in with himself or locked out with *them*?

Was this place really as much of a hellhole as Miriam made it out to be?

Was this "wall" really as safe as she claimed?

Was it even real?

Hayden turned. Walked through the door in front. The light of the prison contrasted with the dull, gloominess of the corridor.

"Just up ahead. A few people waiting in there for you. Cheers for being... well, decent company. I've met worse."

Hayden saw it.

He saw the windows on his left. Dusty. Inside, old CRT screens. Looked like they hadn't been switched on in years.

The corridor.

The corridor Miriam told him to do it in.

To take Tim out.

Take his keys.

Get back to her and help her escape.

"Well, go on," Tim said, chuckling. "We're not attached at the waist, thank the Lord. Just ahead. Through the next door."

Nausea built inside Hayden. Tim's voice sounded so loud. He felt the change in air temperature hit him acutely. The tastes in his dry mouth grew more intense.

He reached into his pocket.

Reached for the sharpened piece of tile.

Either put it through Tim's neck and get out of this place.

Or walk on and survive.

Walk on and survive.

Walk on and...

"Oh," Tim said. "Almost forgot. Summat you were s'posed to do before you got to induction. Ain't that right, number seven?"

Hayden turned around.

He couldn't say a word in response.

Tim was pointing a pistol at him.

He wasn't smiling anymore.

"Drop that weapon of yours and kick it over here before I fill you with lead. You've been ratted out, you scheming sonofabitch."

CHAPTER ELEVEN

"Go on, number seven. Make this nice and easy for yourself. Roll the fucking weapon over this way."

Hayden stared into Tim's glaring eyes. He couldn't speak. He didn't know what to say, just that he wanted to go back to his cell, to hide. Fuck. Miriam. She'd double-crossed him. He'd taken the fucking tile and she'd double-crossed him.

"It—it's not what it looks like," Hayden started.

Tim stepped closer to Hayden. "I don't give a ruddy damn what it looks like. Your cellmate told me about that weapon of yours."

"She—she gave it to me!"

"Oh I bet she did," Tim said. "I bet she did. Just like you're gonna give it to me right now. Then we'll have a talk with management. A proper talk. How's that sound?"

Everything moved so quickly it didn't seem like it was real. Hayden hadn't asked to be in this place. He'd tried to get the hell away from Thomas' group when they got to Danny's with their truck. Fuck. He should never have gone back to Danny's. Should've stayed well away. Away from the past. Away from everyone. Because digging up demons just created new ones.

He saw that now. Saw it clearly.

Pity it was already too late.

"I'm gonna count to five. If you haven't given me that weapon of yours, I'll shoot you. We can say it's self-defence. Nobody'll bat an eyelid. One."

"I swear, I took it because—"

"Two."

Hayden's heart raced.

"Three."

He didn't have a choice. He didn't have a fucking choice.

"Four."

"Okay! Okay." Hayden lifted the sharpened piece of tile from his pocket. He lifted his hand. The object felt alien between his fingers.

Tim nodded. "Now slide it across the floor."

Hayden gulped. "I'm telling you, this isn't what it—"

"Slide it across the fucking floor!"

Tim's booming voice rattled Hayden's body.

He had no choice.

He lowered down. Slid the tile across the floor. And as it drifted away, he saw all hope disappearing. All hope of ever getting out of this place. All hope of surviving. Hell. Maybe that wasn't such a bad thing. Miriam had set him up for whatever reason, so there obviously was no North-South divide. It was all bullshit.

Still a world of nothing.

A world of imprisonment, whether you were outside or in.

No point fighting. Not anymore.

He looked up at Tim. His gun was lowered now. Hayden saw him smiling as he lifted the tile.

"Good," Tim said.

He raised his gun again.

Pointed it at Hayden.

"We can still call it self-defence."

Hayden squeezed his eyes shut.
Waited for the bullet to split his skull.
It didn't.
He heard a thud. Heard some struggling.
A thud? Why would there be a thud? What was the noise?
He opened his eyes.
Peeked at where Tim stood.
Tim was on his knees.
Blood rolled down his face from a crack in his skull.
He fell face flat in a pool of his own blood.
Hayden stared at Tim. Mouth open. Unable to speak.
"Sorry how that had to play out," someone said.
Hayden glanced over the top of Tim's fallen body. He'd been so stunned that he didn't even clock anyone else was here with them.

He saw a woman. Chocolate brown hair. Short, probably little over five foot. Bright blue eyes. Plump lips.

She was holding a fire axe.

"Pleasure to meet you, 'Hayden'," she said. "Now come on. I don't have long."

She ran past Hayden in the opposite direction to the canteen. Disappeared into one of the old offices before Hayden could even ask who she was.

But he knew who she was.

He recognised her voice clearly.

Miriam.

Hayden followed her through into the old office. Saw her rushing around the place, kicking up dust with every step.

"Must be around here somewhere," she said.

"What... How did you—"

"Sorry you had to do that. Again. Really. I knew Tim was coming. Needed to get him out the way fast somehow. That'll teach him to lean back against the cell doors with his master key handy. Well, it won't. But it's a shame. He was a decent guy. I really believe that. Shit. It's here."

She reached a panel on the wall. Flipped it open, smile on her face.

"You killed him," Hayden said.

Miriam turned. Pinched expression on her face. "Seriously. Don't give me that crap. Like you've never killed anyone to make it this far. Anyway, go back to your cell if it's what you really want. You've played your part. Nobody'll be bothered about you when me and my people disappear. Seriously."

Hayden watched Miriam turn the key. "The... the wall. In the south. Is that..."

"Real? Course it's real. Everything I told you is real. Except for your little distraction mission. But that kind of worked out for the best in the end, right?"

"Depends what you mean by 'best'."

Miriam walked away from the panel on the wall. Outside the cells, Hayden heard the collective echo of metal rattling open.

"Look," Miriam said, squaring up to Hayden, as well as a five-foot woman could square up to anyone. "If you aren't sure about following me, don't follow me. If you really are as fucking cynical as I think you are, stay here. Rot in here. You'll probably be a hell of a lot safer."

She walked past Hayden. Towards the corridor. Crouched down and took Tim's gun from his fingers, which still looked tense.

"What if... what if I join you?"

Miriam turned. Looked back at Hayden. Behind the canteen door, he could hear cries and shouts. Mostly shouts of joy. Footsteps clanging against the corridors, against the metal staircase. "I'd appreciate a hand, in all truth. We could use all the help we can get. But if you aren't up for it... you know what you have to do."

Hayden listened to the footsteps. Listened to the people

escaping their cells. He knew he didn't have long to make a decision. He knew he didn't have long to make his choice.

Stay in here. Be safe. Be alone.

Or leave this place.

Get out.

Be free again.

And what Miriam said. About the wall in the south...

No.

That was a pipe dream.

The priority was getting out of this place.

"Come on," Miriam said. "You're coming out this door one way or—"

An alarm sounded from above.

"Everyone on the ground this fucking second!"

Gunfire rattled through the prison.

Hayden thought it was just for show until he saw the blood.

The guards stepped into the prison from upstairs. Firing bullets into everyone still standing. Putting them down like this was all just some kind of game. Painting the walls red.

"Looks like the guards have made your choice for you, Hayden," Miriam said. "Any good with a fire axe?"

She handed the axe to him.

He looked down at it. Looked at her. A person. A person showing trust in him. Showing confidence in him.

He didn't like it.

But he didn't have a choice.

So he took the axe.

The alarm rattling above.

The gunshots peppering through the prison.

Miriam smiled. "Come on. Better get escaping this place."

CHAPTER TWELVE

"On my count," Miriam said. "Three. Two. One. Let's go."

Hayden didn't want to follow Miriam out of the door towards the canteen. He didn't want to throw himself into a battleground. He could hear bullets flying through the prison. Could see people launching themselves at guards, taking them down. And he didn't want to be a part of that. It felt unnatural. Like walking across hot coals.

He knew he was walking towards his own death.

He knew he was risking everything.

But he didn't have a choice. Not anymore.

He just needed to get the hell out of this place.

He crouched down. Squeezed the axe tight in his hand. The guards were on the top level. A few people had made it down the stairs, some of them alive, most of them now dead. A man held onto his bleeding chest, looked up at Miriam. Hayden thought he saw him nod at her like they recognised one another.

And then he heard gunshots crack the tiles on his right.

Hayden launched himself out of the way of them. Ran under the stairs, following Miriam's every step. He saw the others gathering around him, around Miriam, like they were both some kind of leaders.

Nausea built at this fact more than the gunshots thudding in his direction.

Because he knew what happened when he led.

Bad things happened.

"We need to make a break up the stairs."

"That's suicide," someone shouted.

"I know it is, Jack. I know. But we don't have much of a choice right now. Not if we want to get out of here."

Jack shook his head. He had long, dark hair, cracked glasses perched on the bridge of his nose. "Hope you know what you're doing, Miriam."

She smiled at Jack. Tutted. "When have I ever let you down?"

And then she stepped out and raised her hands.

"Don't shoot!" she said.

The guards turned around. Four of them. Pointed their guns right down at her.

"Drop your weapon—"

"You don't want to kill me, Robert. And I don't want to kill you." She walked up the stairs, slowly. Hayden stayed put. So too did everyone else. "We get along, you and me."

The guard called Robert visibly blushed, clearing his throat. "Don't—don't make me shoot you."

"I won't. As long as you let us go back to our cells. Enough people have died here to prove your point. More than enough. Okay?"

Robert fidgeted. The rest of the guards just watched. "I—I need you to lower your weapon, Miri... number thirty-six."

"And I will," she said. "I'm doing that right this second, see. Now you lower yours too. All of you. Please. Nobody else has to die here. We get the message. This is over."

She dropped the gun.

It fell down the staircase.

Landed right at the foot of it.

Just inches away from Hayden.

Hayden stared at it. He knew why it was there. What Miriam wanted him to do. She hadn't told him, but that had to be the plan.

Take the gun.

Shoot the guards.

Get it done with and get out of here.

"The—the rest of you," Robert said. "The rest of your people."

"You shot my people, Robert. You shot so many people. Surely that's not your order? Surely that's not what 'Salvation' is all about?"

Robert cleared his throat again. "I... We need to—to maintain order."

"And you can't maintain order by shooting," Miriam said, emphasis on the shooting.

She'd made her hint perfectly clear.

Hayden knew exactly what she wanted him to do. What they needed to do.

But he froze.

The flashbacks replayed in his eyes. The people he'd let down. The people he'd lost. All because he'd stepped up. All because he'd taken some form of leadership. All because of confidence he'd shown. Responsibility he'd shown.

And he saw a potential sequence of events playing out in front of him once more.

Grabbing the gun.

Shooting the guards.

Miriam dying in the crossfire.

He couldn't do that. Couldn't risk anyone else's life. Couldn't—

"Are you gonna grab that gun or what?" a woman to Hayden's left whispered.

He snapped out of his thoughts. Looked at the gun. Heart pounding. Chest tightening.

He knew what he had to do.

He knew he had to get to it.

He just...

"Fuck it."

The long-haired guy called Jack stepped out from behind Hayden.

Grabbed the gun.

Fired up at the guards.

Hayden didn't see what happened. He heard a lot of gunfire. Heard a lot of shouts. Heard struggling, heard people in pain.

And then he saw blood splatter out of Jack's chest.

Out of his knees.

Out of his neck.

Gunfire peppering down the staircase.

Knocking Jack to the floor as he kept on firing the emptied gun.

Then, silence.

Silence, but for the unending alarm.

The aftermath of the gunfire echoed around the prison. Hayden stared at Jack's motionless body, his arms and legs shaking.

That could've been him.

That should've been him.

Stepping in to try and save others.

Putting his own life on the line to save many more lives.

He peeked out from under the staircase. He didn't want to see what was at the top of the stairs. He didn't want to see Miriam's dead body. He didn't want to see a guard there waiting for him.

But he had to.

He had to look.

He had to know.

He moved his head further around the staircase.

Miriam looked back down the stairs. Pale-faced. Staring at Jack.

Her face was covered in blood.

Around her, the guards were dead.

"Miriam?" Hayden muttered.

She saw him emerge from under the stairs. The rest of the prisoners followed Hayden. Some of them—the survivors—wandered over towards Miriam. An army. An army of prisoners ready to escape.

She blinked. Those blue, watery eyes of hers blinked. Like she was stuck in a daze. Couldn't believe what'd just happened. What she'd just witnessed.

"Come on," she said.

Hayden watched the group emerge from behind him. Saw a few harsh squints in his direction.

He knew why.

He'd not stepped up.

He'd let Jack step up, and he'd let Jack die.

He took a deep breath, the silhouettes of his mind returning to remind him of all the things he'd done, all he'd lost.

And then he walked out from under the staircase.

Followed Miriam's group up the steps.

Away from the prison.

Away from everything.

CHAPTER THIRTEEN

The end of the world and a cold Cobra beer still tasted just as delicious to Terrance Schumer as it always used to.

He leaned back in his reclining chair, eyes closed, just letting the taste of the beer invade his senses. He took deep breaths in, then exhaled, then took deep breaths in again. Meditation. A trick he'd learned years ago. Something to ease the tension whenever he needed to.

He needed to ease the tension a lot these days.

He let memories exit his mind. Let all thoughts and opinions slip away as he stared up into the darkness of his closed eyelids. He knew it was late afternoon on a... Tuesday? Damn. He was forgetting the days. Losing track of them.

But the days didn't matter.

Not when he meditated.

All that mattered?

The now.

Peace.

As he swallowed the beer—not technically a meditation essential, but something that undoubtedly helped—he couldn't help but think about just how similar his life was now to how it was before the country collapsed. Before the world collapsed. He still had his beer. He still had his meditation. He still had his peace.

The only thing he no longer had was his wife, Anantha.

His daughter, Dawn.

A lump swelled in his throat when Dawn entered his mind. Little Dawn. Mousy hair. Cute little button nose. Poor kid. This wasn't a world for her. Wasn't a world for anyone.

But he knew he was one of the lucky ones. Knew he was one of the fortunate survivors.

One of the future.

He had to play his part. He had to follow his duty.

The world required it of him.

Required it of—

A knock on the door snapped him out of his meditation. He opened his eyes. The bright spring sunlight shone in through the window. His room had a blue-ish tinge to it, as was always the case after meditation.

That knock.

That knock at the door again.

"Alright," Terrance said, putting his Cobra to one side and climbing off his recliner. Who wanted him at this time anyway? He was specific when he told people not to interrupt him during the hours of four and five. He thought he'd made himself clear. Very clear.

He coughed, ignoring the dizziness as he walked. Unlocked the wooden door, turned the handle.

Luis stood outside. He was short. Ruffled dark hair. Beady brown eyes. Olive skin underneath his thick black beard.

He looked concerned.

"What's wrong?"

Luis glanced away from Terrance. "I—I'm sorry to disturb you Mr Schumer but I—"

"Woah. Slow down. Slow it right down. What's the problem?"

Luis closed his eyes. Took a calming breath. Opened them again and looked right at Terrance. "It's the Crewe facility."

"What about the Crewe facility?"

"We... We lost contact. Something happened there. Last thing I heard on the system was something about a breach. An escape."

"How many?"

Luis' face twitched. "I think... I think all of them. All the ones who survived. It's weird. The people we had working there. Something happened. They just went... silent."

Terrance's stomach sank. He shook his head. Walked over to the large window at the far side of his room. "So we've got another Luton on our hands."

"They might not know," Luis said, walking after Terrance even though he hadn't been invited in. Brave. Bold. "The citizens there. They might not know. About this place."

Terrance stopped at the window. Looked out at the view. The beautiful view. "Oh, they'll know."

In the distance, from his high-rise apartment block, he saw the city beneath. Saw the streets. The houses. Families. Normal life. That's what they'd strived for. All along, that's what he'd been tasked with creating. Part of his position. His position as the Minister of New Britain. A responsibility he'd been handed years ago, when he just worked as an MP in government. He never thought he'd see the day where an emergency election was called in. Where he was forced to actually lead a group of people. A society. A country.

But he stood here. Looked out at the city. Looked out at his people.

It wasn't a dream.

It was real.

It was happening.

"Got some more incoming, too. From the east."

"And nobody thought to pick them up? You know as well as I do how bustling the city is right now."

"It's not as easy as just picking people up. People see this place and they aren't as willing. We can take them to redistribution centres but it just... well, what happened at Crewe. What happened in Luton. Those things happen. And then when those people get out, they know about this place. People living here, they let the migrants in. Let them share their food. Share their warmth. Sorry, but I think... I think this place is getting unsustainable."

Unsustainable.

The word made Terrance's face twitch.

He turned away from the window. Looked right back at Luis. "You say there's another group incoming. How many?"

Luis puffed out his lips. "Five hundred to a thousand."

Terrance shook his head. "Five-hundred to..."

"We can always try the alternative method. The backup plan. You know."

Terrance thought about Luis' words. He didn't like considering the backup plan. It wasn't ideal. It was reckless. And it ran a very real risk of backfiring on his entire leadership. A risk he wasn't sure he was willing to take.

But a risk he'd have to contemplate. Eventually.

He looked back at the window. Looked out at his beautiful world.

"We allow the migrants inside. Monitor the situation. For now."

Terrance heard Luis' voice crackle like he was going to say something else.

And then he sighed. Nodded. "Very well, Mr Schumer."

He walked away from the window. Left Terrance to look outside.

"I do envy your view sometimes, sir."

Terrance smiled. "I'm a lucky man."

"We're all lucky men, I guess."

"Yes. Yes, we are."

Luis walked out of Terrance's room. Closed the door behind him.

Terrance thought about returning to his meditation. Thought about picking it up again, right here, right now.

Instead, he looked out at the city.

Looked out at the streets.

Looked out at the barbed fences.

Looked out at the towering wall.

The border between the old world and the new world.

The border the migrants were approaching in their droves.

The border he had to control.

Somehow.

CHAPTER FOURTEEN

"We're lucky we only lost one. Coulda been a lot worse."

Hayden walked alongside Miriam. The sun was low, the day merging into night. Still pretty warm, though. Nice weather recently. A day his parents would've called an "early bloomer". Summer rearing its head weeks before its true emergence.

Hayden had always liked summer. Just unfortunate he'd never *really* taken the time to enjoy it in his adult life, choosing booze, pizza, video games and a darkened bedroom as much more suitable company.

He looked at the fields ahead. The Salvation prison was way behind. They'd sprinted out of the gates and found their way out of the place easily. Much easier than he'd expected. Didn't know why. There was something wrong with the place; he knew that much. Something quiet about the place on their way out. Something... off.

The ease the group of twenty-something found getting away from the prison discomforted Hayden. Because no place was quite so easy to flee without a secret.

"Not sure your people agree all that much."

Miriam looked over her shoulder. Looked back at the prisoners, following. "Yeah, well. They're afraid. It's new territory for them out here. And don't call them 'my people'. Please."

"You're a leader. They follow you."

"None of us are leaders," Miriam said. "We're just doing our best to get by."

Hayden glanced back at the following crowd. There were old men. Children. Babies. Weak people. People that didn't seem cut out for this world. "What happens now?"

"What happens now? We walk to the wall. Get to the other side."

"And if you don't like what's on the other side?"

Miriam shook her head. "Whatever's on the other side has to be better than what's on this side."

Hayden thought back to Riversford as he'd first discovered it. "That's not always true."

They walked further. No sign of people. No sign of zombies. The evening chill growing with every step.

"So what's your plan?" Miriam asked.

"My plan?" The question threw Hayden. It wasn't one he was expecting, wasn't one he was prepared for.

Miriam gazed at Hayden with focus. "You didn't seem all that keen on what's on the other side of the wall before you got out the prison."

Hayden broke his stare away from Miriam's blue eyes. "Yeah, well. Figured I'd just..."

A flashback.

To the boy.

The boy.

He thought he saw him in the distance. In the middle of the field.

He thought he saw him with the face of Clarice.

Clarice.

"You okay?"

Miriam's voice snapped Hayden out of his trance. He cleared his throat. Nodded. Heart racing. Chest tightening. "Just... I think I'll go my own way."

Miriam groaned theatrically. "Just go your own way? Your own way to where?"

"To anywhere. The world's our oyster these days. Might as well make the most of it."

"So you've got a death wish then."

"I just..." He stopped. He wasn't sure how much he wanted to open up to Miriam right now. It scared him. The thought of opening up to anyone. "I think it's probably for the best you and your group go your way, and I go mine."

"Because..."

"Because we're different. We've been through different things. Done different things."

Miriam's eyes narrowed. In an instant, Hayden swore he saw the colour drain from her cheeks. "How do you know what I've done? What any of us have done?"

It was a fair question. Who was he to judge? Who was he to jump to conclusions?

As he looked into Miriam's sparkling eyes, her greasy hair hanging long down her back, he tried to picture what she'd been through. What she'd lost. Ultimately, it didn't matter. She'd lost. Everyone had lost. Different stories. Different circumstances, perhaps. But the same result. The same end-game. Always the same.

Death.

An attempt to overcome death.

Maybe even an attempt to be confident in this world. An attempt to lead.

But ultimately, it wasn't the heroes or the leaders that won. It wasn't the fighters who survived.

It was the people who drifted into the background.

The people who became invisible.

They survived.

They walked further, through longer grass. Passed abandoned farms. Empty cars. The night drew in. They'd need to find somewhere to rest soon. Somewhere to stay.

"You not a bit curious?"

"About?"

"The wall. What's on the other side of it."

Hayden thought about it. He was. Of course he was. "I just don't know whether it's for me right now."

"Because you're scared of screwing someone over again?"

Hayden looked back at Miriam. His cheeks flared up. What was she saying? How did she...

"Hold up," Miriam said. She walked back towards the group. Only then did Hayden notice the old man spluttering, coughing. When he turned, he noticed the man spewing up blood. Shaking. Really struggling.

"Gonna need to stop soon," Miriam called. "Harold can't take much more walking. See those cattle stables up ahead? That's where we stay. Okay. Let's get moving."

Hayden walked with the group, Harold continuing to splutter. When they reached the stables, it was dark. He kept his guard up when he arrived because he noticed the smell of rot, the buzzing of flies.

"Grim," Miriam said. The smell and the flies swarmed the dead cows lying in the first few enclosures. But there was no movement. No sign of life. Or death. That was a relief.

The group settled into an enclosure each. And as Hayden stood by the door, he heard laughter. He heard bedtime stories being muttered from parents to children. He heard tears. Yawns. He heard a kind of normality. A fighting against the odds.

He heard togetherness.

But it was all through a lens. Through a dirty lens that he wasn't sure he'd ever clean.

No. He *knew* he'd never clean.

"You staying for the night at least?" Miriam asked.

Hayden jumped. She'd appeared out of nowhere. Leaned on the opposite side of the opening, looked out at her people.

"Suppose I could do with a nap," Hayden said.

"It's normal to be scared," Miriam said. "We're all scared. But you can't let what's happened change you going forward. We've all done shitty things. We've all lost some things. But it's how we react to it. How we fight. That's what keeps us going. That's what keeps us important."

Hayden nodded. Miriam's words bounced around Hayden's head, abstract concepts, ideas that were difficult to tie down. "It must be nice. Having your view of the world."

Miriam smiled. "And it must be fucking grim having your view of the world. Gimme a sec. Gotta use the khazi. Wherever that may be."

She punched Hayden on his left arm. He winced. But it felt kind of strange. Kind of... nice.

He watched Miriam walk towards the other side of the cattle barn. Towards the sheltered area. And he thought about what she said. About it being normal to be scared. About staying strong in the face of... well, in the face of everything. About the importance of people. Surviving. Together.

He waited until she disappeared.

A painful lump swelled in his throat.

He took one final look at the cattle barn full of people.

Then, he turned away and disappeared into the night.

CHAPTER FIFTEEN

Hayden watched the blood drip down his shaking hands, cover the floor of the barn.

If only he'd made the decision to return sooner, maybe things would've been different.

IT STARTED when he walked away into the night. The darkness was thick and suffocating. The wind was strong, which Hayden never liked. The wind always made things move; made it look like figures were following him, chasing him, pursuing him.

Constantly on edge. No respite. No relaxing.

Just the way of the world now.

Something that came with the territory of surviving alone.

He listened to his footsteps on the gravel, his heartbeat racing in his chest. But deep inside, as he climbed the hill, eyes just about adjusting to the moonlight, it was the voices of the people he'd met that echoed in his ears. The memory of Miriam. Of how she'd spoken. Of how she'd spoken to him like she'd known him for years.

Then she'd walked away from him temporarily, and he'd walked away from her permanently.

A taste of nausea built in his mouth. He knew he was wrong for walking away without saying goodbye. But he'd done what he'd done because there was no future for him with that group. There was no future for him with any group. Because when he was with groups, people died. Usually because of him.

He didn't want to lose anyone else.

He didn't want to be responsible for any more death.

So he walked away.

His feet were chapped, blistered. He couldn't walk much more. He'd have to find somewhere to rest eventually. But with every pained step, the memory of Miriam filled his mind.

The wall.

The boundary between the north and the south.

A safe place beyond it.

He still wasn't sure whether to believe it. But he'd overheard plenty of the other refugees discussing it in the background. Heard the rumours. The rumours of a good world beyond. A world where people survived. Where they led relatively normal lives.

But as Hayden walked into the dark, something unsettled him about that supposed normality. It didn't seem right. Didn't fit right. The world out here was dying, close to dead. And yet he was supposed to just crawl behind a wall and act like everything was normal, everything was fine?

He wasn't sure he could do that. He wasn't sure he could pretend. Not after everything that'd happened.

He heard a groan up ahead. A throaty, guttural cry. It didn't scare him. Didn't unsettle him. Not anymore. Zombies were just a part of the background now. Just a part of the world. Really, they represented the world. Hungry. Dying. Desperate.

In a way, he pitied them.

Hayden lifted the fire axe he'd found on his way down here

and readied himself to attack the zombie. To put it down. Put it out of its misery. He couldn't see it yet. And admittedly, it was weird that a lone straggler just happened to be walking along out here in the countryside.

There was something absurd about it. Something abnormal. Something...

He felt the tightness around his left arm out of nowhere.

He swung around. Smacked the zombie right across its face with the axe.

He couldn't see it properly. Just that it was short-haired. Smaller than him.

Blood drooling down its chewed up face.

Hayden hit it again. Harder this time, aiming for the next. But the zombie just kept its grip. And as Hayden stood there fighting, he got a flash of something. A momentary flash in his mind.

Why are you still fighting?

The thoughts came thick and fast, all in the space of a moment.

If you're fighting to survive, then why?

What is your plan?

What is your end game?

Do you really want to be alone forever?

And as the zombie lurched for his shoulder, the answer invaded his thoughts. Screamed around his mind.

No.

He didn't want to be alone.

He wanted to be safe. Somewhere safe.

He wanted the people he'd escaped the prison with.

He wanted Miriam.

He smacked the zombie across its neck. Heard its spine split on contact.

The zombie tightened its grip for a second. Started shaking, convoluting, spitting out blood.

And then its muscles went limp and it fell to the ground.

Hayden stood there in the moonlight, which had burned through the clouds completely now. He listened to the wind brush against the trees. The light rain falling from the clouds above, making him even colder than he already was.

No.

He didn't want to be alone.

He wanted to be in company.

He wanted to see what was on the other side of that wall.

He wanted Miriam's group.

He turned back. Ran down the hill, back down the road that led to the farm. He ran for hours. Ran right into the brightening sky, the rising sun. Nothing stopped him. Not the pain in his legs. Not the bursting blisters on his feet. The knowledge of what he'd walked away from chewed at him, niggled at him.

He was going back.

Back to Miriam.

Back to her people.

He was going back to the farm.

Back to join them.

Back to...

He stopped. Stopped when he exited the woods. When he saw the hills leading down towards the farm, which was a few miles down the road.

The first thing he noticed was the smell.

Then the sounds.

The mass of buzzing flies.

The hundreds of dead footsteps.

His throat tightened up. He couldn't think. Couldn't comprehend what he was seeing.

Just that a mass of dead were swarming towards the farm.

The farm where Miriam and her group were staying.

The farm he'd walked away from.

Getting closer and closer by the second.

CHAPTER SIXTEEN

Hayden kept on sprinting when he saw the mass of zombies approaching the farm, approaching the cattle barn.

He wasn't sure how many there were exactly. At least fifty. He couldn't be sure where they'd come from. He definitely hadn't encountered them on his walk away from the farm.

Didn't really matter. All that mattered was they were here now.

They were here, and they were approaching the farm.

He had to get to Miriam and the group before the zombies did.

He had to warn them.

He had to help them.

He'd run so far, he couldn't feel his legs anymore. His chest was tight, getting tighter by the second. He'd struggled with intermittent asthma as a kid. Told he had it, and then told he didn't have it, then told he did have it all over again. He knew he could do with an inhaler right now. Something to ease his breathing. To loosen his chest.

No.

He didn't have that luxury.

All he could do was focus.

All he could do was run.

He heard the moans of the infected getting louder the closer he got to the farm. At the current speed they were walking on the road to the left, he'd get there before them. Just.

But he couldn't afford to slow down. Couldn't afford to lower his pace.

He wasn't sure he could hold this up much longer.

He kept his focus ahead. Kept it on the farm. On the cattle barns. He looked for movement. Looked for signs of life. A sign that Miriam and her group were still in there. That they were okay.

Or maybe it'd be better if they'd left. Maybe it'd be better if they'd gone.

His fist tightened around the axe.

No.

He wanted them to be there.

He wanted to help them.

He wanted to be a part of their group...

He saw the zombies drifting closer to the barn as he approached. A few of them turned. Looked at him across the field. Shit. They'd definitely keep moving to the farm now. He was leading them right fucking there. Just the help Miriam and her group needed. The final twist of the knife after turning his back on them.

No!

He could do this.

He could make it.

He could help...

When he entered the farmyard, he saw movement.

Inside the cattle barn.

And from the sluggish manner of movement, from the

droning groans from the back of their throat, he knew exactly what kind of movement it was.

Zombie movement.

He lowered the axe. Crept towards the cattle barn entrance. Fuck. No. No. The dead couldn't have made it here already. It explained why the horde of infected was drifting towards the cattle barn, though. Hayden didn't know much about the nature of the dead, but they seemed to prefer working in groups. They were drawn together like ants. Like some kind of signal emitting from them, magnetising them.

Hayden heard the cries of the zombies in the distance. Smelled them getting closer to the cattle barn, closer to him.

But he kept his focus on the cattle barn itself.

On the footsteps drifting along the ground.

The low rumble emitting from the zombie's throat.

He stepped around the cattle barn door. Looked inside.

He tried to keep him calm. Tried to keep his composure.

But when he saw the people lying dead on the cattle barn floor, he couldn't.

Not when he saw Harold—the man who'd been in a bad way earlier—crouching over a young girl, chewing on her neck.

Not when he saw an old man's intestines resting in his hands, a shocked look on his greying face.

Not when he saw the eight other zombies walking around the cattle barn.

Hayden's chest tightened. He gripped the axe. Miriam's group. They'd reached Miriam's group, and they'd attacked them. They'd fucking attacked them.

He couldn't let the thought go. Couldn't just let it drop.

The people he'd walked away from.

More people he'd failed to protect.

Gone.

Hayden banged the axe against the metal door, the sound of the mass of zombies getting closer.

The zombies inside the barn lifted their heads. The coughing man moved away from the girl he was chewing, innards dangling down his chin.

He looked at Hayden with empty eyes.

All of them looked at Hayden with empty eyes.

Then, they walked towards him.

Hayden didn't give them any time to act. Didn't give them any chance to grab him.

He just swung the axe at the neck of the first zombie. A middle-aged guy with dark curly hair. One he recognised from the survivors.

Cracked his neck, put him down.

He swung the axe into the neck of a skinny ginger boy, too. He went down much easier. But it was always more difficult dealing with the younger zombies, from a moral standpoint.

The sound of that little snarl—that obvious child snarl—was enough to stop anyone with any level of empathy inside right in their tracks.

When the boy fell back onto the barn floor, still snarling despite his neck clinging on by a thread of bone, Hayden rammed the axe across his neck once again.

He took down the rest of the zombies. Took them down, one by one. And as he did, he saw Miriam. Saw her in his mind. Remembered what she'd said. About fighting for something. About keeping on going, doing everything they could, never giving up. Because that's all there was now. That's what made them human.

They fought for each other.

And he'd walked away.

He'd walked away and more people had died.

He'd fucking walked away thinking he was doing the right thing, and still, this happened.

He cracked the axe through Harold's balding skull. Beat him repeatedly until his head was nothing more than a splatter of brain and bone on the barn floor. He kept on trying to drag himself up, trying to clutch at Hayden.

Hayden spat on him, rage building up inside. The zombies. The zombies had taken so much away from him. They'd taken everything away from him. They had to pay.

They all had to fucking pay.

He cracked the axe across the neck of the final zombie.

Then, when silence filled the cattle barn, he fell to his knees.

He crouched there, silent. Watched the blood drip down his shaking hands, cover the floor of the barn.

If only he'd made the decision to return sooner, maybe things would've been different. Maybe he could've helped. Or... fuck. At least he would've died fighting with them. At least he would've died for something.

At least he wouldn't have died alone.

Like he was destined to.

Like he'd fucking chosen.

He squeezed his eyes shut. Smelled the zombies outside closing in on the barn, heard their footsteps getting closer.

If only he had the confidence.

If only he had the courage.

The courage to fight.

The courage he'd once had. But the courage that'd been taken away from him. Stripped away from him. Robbed.

He let all thoughts drift from his mind. Let himself forget everything, everyone, as the zombies' footsteps started to fill the yard outside, as they approached the cattle barn doors.

And then he heard a click.

Felt something hard press into the back of his head.

"Drop that axe and stand up. Slowly."

CHAPTER SEVENTEEN

"Drop the axe and stand up. Slowly."

Hayden listened to the voice over his shoulder. He stared at the blood in front of him. The blood of the zombies he'd taken down. Refugees. Miriam's group. Or rather, *former members* of Miriam's group. Before the zombies attacked them. Before they turned.

From outside, he heard the zombies walking across the yard. They were so close. Whoever this group were—whoever it was holding a gun to his head—they were going to die in here too. "We—we need to get out or—"

"Like you got out last time?" a woman muttered. "Like you ran away?"

Hayden turned. The voice. He recognised the voice.

Behind him, behind the man holding a gun to his head, Hayden saw Miriam.

His heart fluttered. "You."

"Yes, me." She turned around. Swung the pipe against the neck of an oncoming zombie. Pushed it away. More zombies approaching, drifting in, escaping the falling rain. "You think you can just wander in and out of our company whenever you fancy it?"

"Miriam, I—"

The gun pressed further into the back of his head.

"What do you want?" Miriam asked. Two more zombies approached, flesh dangling off their withered bones.

"I... I want to join you. Join your group."

Miriam smiled. She attacked the first of the zombies, another member of the group—an Asian guy called Prem—took down the other. "Which is why you ran away from us. Which is why Harold got bit."

"I was afraid."

"How many more times are you gonna be afraid?"

Hayden watched the rest of the group fight off the zombies. They couldn't take them all on. And he wasn't exactly safe, crouched here in the middle of the barn.

"I don't know," Hayden answered honestly. "But I want to give this a shot. I want to... to give it a try. I want to help you."

Miriam backed away from the door. So too did more of her people. They watched as zombies crowded the entrance. No way out through that door now. No fucking chance.

"Do you want to help us? Really? Or do you just want to help yourself?"

Hayden wanted to tell Miriam all the things he'd done. All the lives he'd saved. Where he'd come from—a wimp. A fucking wimp with no purpose in life. To a fighter. To a leader.

He wanted to tell her how he'd got to where he was. And why he'd fallen.

But he couldn't.

The man holding the gun to Hayden's head lifted him up. Pushed Hayden towards the back of the barn.

"Everyone out through the back!" Miriam shouted.

They ran. Everyone ran as the zombies swarmed inside,

momentarily distracted by the rotting cows. But not for long. Never for long. Not when there was movement.

Hayden reached the back of the barn. Saw some of the group climbing the wall at the back. Climbing towards an open window. He looked at the people around him. Old people. Children. The young and the fit might be able to make it up there, but the older folk were going to struggle.

He heard a crash. Heard flesh being torn by metal.

He looked around, saw four of the group fighting off the oncoming mass of dead. Miriam included.

All of them putting their lives on the line to protect the weak.

All of them stepping up.

Just like Hayden was supposed to.

He held out a hand to a short old woman with greying hair. "Take my hand. Let me help you up there."

He eased the woman up onto a raised platform of hay. He wasn't exactly the most muscular guy himself. But he had age and... well, moderate fitness on his side. That counted for something.

A shout from behind. One of the guys was surrounded. Swarmed by zombies. Hayden watched the undead wrap their hands around his throat, rip the flesh from his face, crush his skull.

Miriam and the others just kept on fighting.

Kept on holding the undead off.

Kept on doing what they had to do.

Hayden helped another person up. A little girl, no older than six. She was so skinny he could feel every bone in her body as he lifted her onto the hay.

She got up on top of it. She was the last one. Just Miriam and two others now. The two fighting. The two he should be over there helping.

He started to climb towards the window, ease himself outside.

And then he saw Miriam fall over.

Saw the zombies close in on her.

He let go of the window ledge instinctively. Ran over towards Miriam. He couldn't control himself. Just had to get to her. Just had to save her.

He lifted the axe from where he'd dropped it earlier.

Pulled it back.

Swung it across the skull of the first of the dead, their gasps and moans filling the cattle barn.

And then he smacked another across the head.

"Take my hand!"

Miriam glanced up at him. He saw the look in her eyes. That puzzlement. That confusion. And that fear, too. The fear of trusting someone else. But above anything, that fear of trusting Hayden.

He hadn't done anything to earn her trust.

Not until now.

She took his hand.

He pulled her up.

Dragged her out of the reach of more zombies.

Together, they ran towards the barn exit, towards the hay platform, towards the window.

When they'd climbed the hay, Hayden helping Miriam up, he heard a scream. A desperate scream, like a pig being slaughtered.

He looked back.

Saw the two men who'd been with Miriam on the ground.

Teeth ripping open their stomachs.

Undead feasting on their insides.

"Fuck," Miriam said. "Fuck."

Hayden watched the blood spray out of their bodies. He watched, and he knew he'd had a choice. He knew he could've tried to save them.

But Miriam was here.

She was alive.

He'd saved someone.

That was something.
That was a start—
He felt the hay give way.
Felt himself tumble away from the window.
The axe fall beside him.
Towards the oncoming undead below…

CHAPTER EIGHTEEN

"You're heavier than you look, son. You owe me a new hand. And a new back. I can tell you that much."

Hayden walked alongside the group. They'd been walking for hours. So long that, somehow, the day had reached the point of sunset again. It had been another nice day. Bright. Warm. In some ways, it felt like forever since the attack on the cattle barns this morning. In others, it didn't seem long ago at all. Time drifted on, hard to grasp, difficult to comprehend.

Probably something to do with Hayden being amongst company. At last.

He looked to his left. Saw Bob Newton walking beside him. Bob had caught him before he fell into the cattle barn. He was old—mid-sixties, with reddish skin and perfectly white hair—but he was tough. Well built. He was exactly the guy Hayden needed there to catch him back in the barn. Exactly the fortune he required.

"I owe you my life," Hayden said, looking ahead now, ahead at the stretching country lane, at the fields, the trees, the setting sun.

"And yet you wouldn't give me your life, would you?"

"Hmm?"

Bob smiled. Revealed a few teeth were missing. "If you had to put yer life on the line for me. For any of us. You wouldn't do it, would you?"

Hayden looked at the ground. He wasn't sure what exactly to say to Bob. "I... I went back. For—"

"You went back for Miriam, yeah. But you didn't go back for Arnold. You didn't go back for Nick."

"I couldn't save them all. I would've, but I..."

"You chose Miriam. And hell, son. I don't blame you. She's a pretty girl. About your age. If I had the balls, I'd probably do the same."

Hayden felt his cheeks heating up. He looked ahead at Miriam. Short, but standing tall as she led the group on, on towards the wall, towards whatever hid behind it. Did Bob have a point? Did saving Miriam have something to do with how attractive she was?

No. He wasn't that shallow. He couldn't be that shallow."

Bob coughed. Leaned over, spluttered onto the grass.

"You okay?" Hayden asked.

Bob wiped his mouth. Nodded. His eyes were bloodshot, watery. "Damned cough. Had it since back at Salvation. Must've been some kind of bug goin' round. Doesn't surprise me. Absolute shithole."

Hayden took a few steps ahead of Bob. Didn't want to get too close.

The air smelled sweet, another sign of the oncoming summer. And as Hayden walked with Bob, walked with the rest of the group, he tried to picture himself last summer. Locked away in his room. Life going nowhere. Probably playing some shitty video game or other.

And now he was here.

Now he was fighting.

Just without anyone to fight for.

"Something weird happened. Back there."

Hayden turned back to Bob. The tone of his voice had changed. His eyes were glassy. "What do you mean?"

Bob sniffed up. "Harold. He turned. But I didn't see anyone bite him. Didn't see a thing like that."

"He must've been bitten. He was one of the dead."

"Do you really believe that?"

"Believe... believe what?"

Bob stared Hayden right in the eye for a few seconds. Then he smiled. Shook his head. "You know what the problem with you is?"

"I thought we were talking about—"

"You can't let go of the past."

Hayden watched Bob walk ahead of him. The sky was red with the setting sun. They'd have to find somewhere else to rest. Somewhere else to stay for the night. He didn't know how far they were from the wall. Didn't know where it started.

Only that he was going along with them.

Going along with them because it's what he had to do.

It was his only choice.

"What do you know about my past?" Bob asked.

"I know I've been through shit in my life. I know I've made mistakes. I've lost people. Found people. Lost 'em again. But I don't frigging mope about the mistakes I've made. I don't give up on life just cause things ain't as rosy as they once were. I just move on. Find new people. 'Cause that's what matters, Hayden. That's what matters more than anything."

Hayden hung on. Waited for him to continue.

When he didn't, he had to ask the question. "What matters?"

Bob raised his arms. Smiled. "People. That's what matters. Doesn't matter whether we're out here or behind a wall. What matters is we're together. That we're confident. That we fight. That we have goals, routines, ambitions."

"Hard to have ambition in a world like this."

Bob waved a hand. Tutted. "Oh, enough. Enough with yer negative bullcrap. It's catching."

He nudged Hayden in his left arm. Hayden winced.

"Sorry," Bob said. "The needle mark. Forget how bad it stings sometimes."

Hayden didn't know what Bob was talking about at first.

Not until Bob rolled up his white sleeve, revealed the seeping red mark on his right arm.

"Shit. Is that from..."

"The needle back at Salvation," Bob said, nodding. "Always a fucker at reacting to needles. Yours okay?"

Said a lot that Hayden forgot he'd even been injected. He pulled back his sleeve. Not a sign of it. Not a prick. "Yeah. Mine's okay. But I'm sure yours will be—"

Bob started coughing again. Started spluttering. This time, his coughs were violent.

They reminded Hayden of Harold's coughs.

Harold who turned.

Harold, who Bob claimed he hadn't seen bitten.

But more than anything, Hayden couldn't help but think of Little Tim back at Riversford.

"Are you okay?"

"Fine," Bob said. Although he looked far from it. Blood dripped out of both nostrils. His skin had turned pale. "You... you walk on. Go chat with Miriam. We're only young once, and all that. Think you need a bit of a conversation, too. Bit of a bonding."

"Are you sure you'll—"

"Go on! Shoo!"

Bob waved his hand, gesturing Hayden to leave. And Hayden complied. He felt reluctant about complying. Reluctant about leaving Bob alone. He liked Bob. Seemed a nice guy. One of the few group members who actually had the time of day for him.

He walked on. Walked towards Miriam. Heart thumping. Every muscle in his body tensing for reasons he couldn't explain.

"Just remember what's important in life," Bob called.

Hayden looked back.

Saw Bob smiling at him at the rear of the group. Covering his bleeding nostrils.

Hayden nodded back at him. Smiled. "People."

"People," Bob repeated.

Hayden turned away from Bob. Looked at the setting sun, the ever-reddening sky.

AT THE BACK of the line, Bob pulled back his sleeve.

Looked at the needle wound.

A sense of dread filled his body.

A sense of dread about what he knew was happening.

Of what he'd have to do.

CHAPTER NINETEEN

The boy was at the window again.

Hayden stood in that corridor. Beneath him, he felt the hands of his family—of those he'd lost—reaching up, grabbing him, trying to drag him below.

He heard their groans. Heard them gasping, growling, just like the undead.

But all he focused on was the boy.

The little boy at the window.

Blood streamed down his face. Drooled from his eyes. His lip was bust. His skin was purple. Flies buzzed around him, their little wings collectively adding up to something much louder, much more intense than any other noise in this reality.

"Why do you always leave me?" the boy sobbed.

Sobbed tears of blood.

Red tears.

Hayden opened his mouth to respond but he couldn't. He felt the vice grip around his throat. The vice grip of teeth.

Only when he looked into the eyes of the monster biting him, he realised it was Miriam.

Miriam, with her dead eyes.

Miriam, joining the rest of the dead.

No. Not Miriam. Not—

"Why do you always leave us?"

The voice was loud. Made the walls shake. And when Hayden looked back over at the boy at the window, he saw his eyes bulging.

Saw them turning blue.

Then...

The boy's eyes burst open.

Blood splattered out of them. Sprayed all over the grey walls of this corridor.

Hayden's family dragged him below and ripped him to—

He woke suddenly. Heart racing. Sweat rolling down his forehead even though it was cool. He took in a few deep breaths. His chest was tight. His muscles, weak.

He was okay. It was just a dream.

Just the same old fucking dream.

He closed his eyes again. Pressed his head against his legs. He couldn't hear any sounds around him but for the creaking of the holiday cabin he was inside. They'd found the place just after dark. Derelict, abandoned. Decent shelter in the middle of some woods. One of those places he'd go on adventure holidays with his family when he was younger.

The creaking floorboards upstairs. Shifting in the breeze, or with the slightest turn of a group member.

Then, lightly, from one of the other rooms, snoring.

He raised his head. Squinted in the darkness. There was a television mounted on the wall at the other side of the room. Said a lot about how much the world had changed that he didn't even think about trying to turn it on. Over to the left of the room, an imitation fireplace. Leaflets spread across the oak table; a high chair propped against it. He wondered who'd stayed here before the turn. Wondered whether they'd found out about it through friends or via that television.

He wondered if they'd found out at all.

There must've been so many people out there who didn't have a fucking clue what was going on. Not that he did—just, being a bit younger, abstract concepts like zombie apocalypses were somewhat more believable. Just somewhat.

But all the old people who'd died. All the terrified children who'd watched their parents stumble towards them.

The feeling of ultimate betrayal when a dad wraps his teeth around his son's neck.

Rips his flesh away.

The sense of paternal idolisation that wouldn't die; not even then.

His thoughts were interrupted when he heard a bang outside.

He jolted upright. Looked around the lounge. A few other group members were in here with him. Sammy. Bradley. People he didn't know as much as others. Still felt detached from most of them. At a distance.

They were fast asleep.

Didn't budge.

Hayden heard something outside again.

Shuffling.

His body tensed. The curtains were partly open, a slither of moonlight seeping in. He had to stand up. He had to close them. He had to do it before whatever was out there looked inside. Before whatever was out there saw him, saw the group.

He stood, knees clicking. Crept over to the curtains. Grabbed them gently. Didn't want to draw any attention to himself, to the house. Didn't know whether it was human or zombie out there.

Didn't really matter.

All that mattered was his silence.

All that mattered was...

He stopped. Hands on the curtains.

Something was out there.

Something... something was lying in the dirt.

He saw the grey hair shining in the moonlight, in the stars, and he recognised the figure right away.

Bob.

He frowned. Stepped away from the window. Bob was hurt. He'd seemed worse for wear earlier. That mark on his arm. Maybe the tetanus shot had reacted badly? He certainly looked hunched up. Like his muscles were tensed. Like his body had tightened.

He had to go out there.

Had to check how he was.

But something slowed Hayden's departure from the house. A feeling. An ill feeling about this entire situation.

Something wasn't right.

He walked out of the lounge, past his sleeping companions. The corridor was dark. No sign of the door being opened. Made the hairs stand on the back of his neck. What other way out of the cabin was there? And why was Bob outside in the first place?

Hayden thought back to the noise he'd heard. The thud.

Like something... dropping.

Hayden swallowed a lump in his dry throat. Maybe something happened upstairs. Maybe Bob fell. Fell out of a window...

No. That was ridiculous. Way too ridiculous.

He remembered what Bob said to him. *"Just remember what's important in life. People."*

The air of finality when he'd said it.

Like he was saying goodbye.

Like he was giving up.

Hayden rushed towards the door of the cabin. Lowered the handle. Stepped out into the cold night breeze.

Seeing Bob lying on his side, legs twisted out of position, made Hayden just want to head back into the cabin. Pretend he hadn't seen Bob. Wake in the morning and act as if everything was normal... until their discovery.

But he knew there was no escape.

He knew there was no walking away. Not again.

So he stepped out into the front yard of the cabin.

Walked closer to Bob, who was perfectly still.

As Hayden got closer, the moonlight shifting from behind a thin film of clouds, he saw the damage to Bob's body. Saw the blood pooling from his skull. Saw his arms twisted in impossible angles, elbow piercing out of his skin.

He saw Bob lying there and he knew it was over. He knew he'd ended his life. For whatever reason, he'd—

Then, he heard a gasp.

He didn't understand it. Didn't know where it came from. Looked around. Peered into the darkness. Zombies. Zombies were here. Zombies were attacking. Zombies were—

Then he heard it again.

This time, he knew exactly where it came from.

Didn't understand it. Didn't want to accept it. But there was no way around it.

Bob's neck twisted around. He looked up at Hayden, crack in his skull.

Looked at Hayden with empty eyes.

With dead eyes.

He snarled. Blood trickled down his cracked teeth. And as Hayden started to step away, back off to the house, he heard something else.

A scream.

A scream from upstairs.

CHAPTER TWENTY

Hayden sprinted into the house, leaving a gasping Bob behind.

He ran through the door. Back into the darkness. He heard the screams upstairs. Upstairs, where Bob had been sleeping. In the rest of the house, he heard footsteps. Panicked voices. Confusion and fear kicking in as the rest of the group awoke.

"The hell's going on?" someone to Hayden's right asked. Bradley.

Hayden looked up the brown-carpeted stairs. Looked up to where he knew he had to go. Where he knew he had to investigate.

"Make sure you all stay close," Hayden said, walking away from Bradley, heading up the stairs.

"But what's—"

"Just lock yourself in the lounge and don't step inside. Not until I know it's clear."

Hayden heard Bradley kick up a fuss. Heard him begin to protest.

But it didn't matter anyway. He was climbing the stairs.

Making his way to the top.

As he climbed, the taste of sick building in his mouth, he thought about these people. This group who'd travelled so far, who'd been through so much. He thought about Miriam. Thought about the efforts she'd gone to in escaping the prison. He thought about what he owed her.

Bob's words. *"Just remember what's important in life. People."*

Bob, lying dead—no, undead—outside the cabin.

Something had happened.

Something happened upstairs.

And now Hayden was about to find out.

He turned onto the top floor of the house to see two people standing by the door. Craig and Deborah. They both stood there, holding on to the handle. Both crying.

"What's happening?" Hayden asked.

They didn't respond. They just stayed by the door. Kept holding on.

Hayden walked towards the door. A musty smell filled the air. Dampness. Sweat. "What's—"

"You don't want to go in there," Deborah said.

Behind the door, Hayden heard the struggling. The screaming had stopped, but there was still movement.

Still something beyond that wooden door.

Something waiting inside.

Hayden stopped by the door. Looked at it. Listened to the silence. He knew what'd probably happened. A zombie had got in there somehow. Bitten Bob. Tossed him out the window. Or maybe he'd tossed himself out the window to protect the others.

No. The blood on his teeth.

He'd bitten someone.

He'd...

"It just... it just happened," Deborah said, her voice shaky. "Out of nowhere. Everything was quiet. Then they just... they just turned."

Hayden looked past Deborah. Looked at the door. The way she said those words. *They just turned.*

It didn't make sense.

It didn't add up.

Something was wrong.

Something was...

He heard a bang against the door. Deborah screamed, tumbled forward.

And then the banging stopped.

The room went quiet.

Hayden stood there. Stood there, heart racing, staring at the wood. He knew what the sensible thing to do would be. Turn around. Walk away. Leave. Each and every one of them.

But he knew he couldn't.

He had to see what was behind this door.

He had to see to understand.

To really believe.

"Hayden! What the fuck's going on?"

The voice from behind made the tension seep from Hayden's body. He turned. Saw Miriam standing there. She was holding a pipe.

Hayden smiled at her. Nodded. He felt bad for feeling relieved at seeing her again. Because something was wrong. Something terrible had happened.

But he couldn't disguise his relief.

He was pleased to see Miriam.

Pleased she was okay.

"They just turned," Deborah repeated, her words growing more slurred.

"Who just—"

"All of them. Bob. Will. Rajiv. One second they were okay. Next second they..."

"Are you saying they were bitten?" Miriam asked.

"No," Hayden said. He turned around. Took the pipe from

Miriam's hand. She didn't put up much of a protest. "No, she isn't saying that at all."

He looked around at the remaining group members, all of them peeking at Hayden, at the door. Fourteen of them. Fourteen of twenty-two.

The other eight, missing.

In this room.

On the ground outside the house.

"If they weren't bitten, then what's this all about?"

Hayden tried not to think back to Riversford as he put a hand on the door handle.

He tried not to think about little Tim Striker.

The way he'd just turned.

Turned, without a bite mark.

Turned out of the blue.

He'd been trying his best not to accept that reality—accept what it might mean for the world—for a long, long time.

He took off his jacket. Covered his face with it. Wasn't sure if it was any good. Wasn't even sure whether his suspicions were right.

But if they were, he couldn't risk it.

He couldn't risk a thing.

He felt the handle reach the end of its turn.

Waited a few seconds. Held his breath.

Then, he pushed the door open.

He heard the creak. Heard it echo right through the rest of the cabin.

The first thing he noticed was the window. Smashed. Specks of blood around the serrated edges of the glass. So that's what'd happened to Bob. Definitely crashed out the window. Poor bastard.

But it was the rest of the figures that Hayden noticed most.

The four figures crouching down on the bedroom floor.

Ripping into three twitching bodies.

The figures of children eating the bodies of adults.

The figures of adults eating the bodies of children.

Hayden heard a few curses behind him. A few gasps as the rusty smell of blood filled his nostrils. But he didn't process them properly. Didn't take them in as he looked back into the room. Back at the group members. The group members who definitely hadn't been bitten. Who'd definitely just... turned.

One of them—Rajiv—lifted his head. A piece of flab from Bhvishya's belly rolled down his chin. He glanced up at Hayden and snarled.

Hayden backed away.

Closed the door.

Held it shut as Rajiv and the rest of the zombies battered at it, tried to get out.

"What now?" Miriam asked.

Hayden stood there. Stood there holding onto the rattling door. Listening to the sounds of the fallen group members. The turned group members. Memories, theories, fears all whizzing around his mind.

Then he stepped away from the door.

Walked towards the stairs.

"Hayden, what—"

"We leave this place," Hayden said. His voice felt unreal, detached from his body. "We get far away from it."

"But what about our dead?" Deborah sobbed.

Hayden didn't have anything to say in return.

As he descended the stairs, all he could think about was Little Tim at Riversford.

All he could think about was his sudden turning.

All he could think about was what this meant. Not just for his group, but for everyone.

What it meant for humanity if the virus really had adapted in the way he feared.

CHAPTER TWENTY-ONE

Terrance Schumer stared out at the crowd and wondered how he'd ever admit what he was about to tell them.

It was 11 a.m. The weather was improving as summer drifted ever closer. Today, the sun beamed down on his balding scalp, making his headache even worse. It was stuffy. Air filled with the smells of cooked meat—meat they'd procured from their farming project. One of the roles many of the early migrants took on. One of the ways to integrate them into their new society beyond the wall. The new world of New Britain.

But as with everything involving the migrants, jobs ran out. The numbers growing ever larger, the dynamics of this new world shifting by the day.

It couldn't go on much longer. Not with New Britain bursting at the seams.

Terrance Schumer looked around at his people from the podium he stood on. He heard their chatter. Their laughter. People who'd lived here from the start mixing with the migrants who'd made their way inside. Beautiful, really. Peace. Real peace.

But nothing lasted forever.

He wished they lived in an ideal world. But they didn't.

And they were about to understand that.

They were about to understand the truth.

The truth they might've feared. The truth some of them might have suspected all along.

The truth that shattered the walls and made this whole crisis all the more real again.

Terrance Schumer cleared his throat. The microphone squeaked. Caught the attention of the crowd.

"I... I don't like changing meeting times. Twelve p.m. is always better for obvious reasons. But I've been left with no choice."

A few eyes narrowed. Terrance Schumer saw the sense growing amongst the crowd. The sense that something was wrong. Something wasn't quite as planned. That this meeting really was different.

If only they knew the full truth.

If only they knew.

Terrance Schumer cleared his throat again. Looked down at the wooden stage on which he stood. People below him. Houses behind him. Houses, apartments, shops. The wall.

But more than anything, he saw his people.

The people who stood by him.

The people who stood by his side no matter what.

The people who'd kept him where he was.

"I didn't want to tell you the full truth. Not until we knew. For certain. Because don't get me wrong. Make no mistake about it. What I'm about to announce changes things. Changes the way we're living. Changes the way we move forward."

The crowd were silent now. Silent, but for a few coughs. Silent, but for the wail of a baby.

Terrance Schumer's eyes started to water. The reality of the situation grew the closer he got to the announcement. He wanted to just spit it out. Wanted to just get the truth out there.

But he couldn't.

He had to build up to it.

He had to be... sensitive.

Or at least, he had to be political.

"For months, we have allowed refugees to walk beyond our walls. We have let them into our community as our own. And rightly so. We're powerful. Perhaps the most powerful stronghold left in Britain right now. We're the only place that can offer true shelter. True refuge. A future."

A few smiles amongst the crowd. Grateful refugees. Proud individuals.

"But some alarming truths have come to light. Something we've suspected for a long time, but only now can confirm."

Terrance Schumer saw the terrified faces. He knew what this would do to him. It'd destroy him. Destroy the trust between them.

But eventually, they'd come crawling back to him.

Because fear was as powerful as trust.

No. Fear was *more* powerful than trust.

"What're you saying?" someone from the back shouted.

Terrance Schumer looked for the shouter. Didn't find them. Didn't have to. Everyone was staring at him. Everyone waiting for his announcement. Waiting for his revelation.

He wiped his sweaty hair back. Taste of vomit in his mouth.

He looked back up at the waiting crowd.

No getting away from it now.

No escaping the truth.

No place to hide.

"The virus. The infection. The one that changed so many of our loved ones. The one that... the one that ravaged our beautiful former country. The one that swallowed our world whole. It's..."

Terrance Schumer saw Luis at the front of the crowd. He saw him nodding. Damned Luis. He'd wanted this all along. This was his method. His idea. The very thing he'd implemented.

The alternative method.

The backup plan.

But as much as Terrance loathed the idea, he knew it was right. He knew it was right for the future of humanity. The future of New Britain.

He knew people had to fall for people to rise.

And that's why he felt no guilt about the decision he'd made to announce the reality.

Not anymore.

"Spit it out!" a woman shouted. Her voice echoed through the silence.

Terrance Schumer closed his eyes.

Swallowed.

Opened them again. Looked out at the crowd.

"I'm sorry to have to announce we're closing the door to new refugees as of this second."

Silence, initially.

Then a few puzzled glances.

Then, in an instant, a roar of questions.

Terrance Schumer watched the pandemonium beneath. Saw angry faces of migrants. Saw frustrated, puzzled looks on those who'd taken them into their homes, into their workplaces.

He listened to the chaos erupt. Listened to it surround him.

Then, he stepped back to the microphone.

"We're closing the gates and we're running a decontamination programme right here in New Britain."

More puzzlement. Bafflement. Everyone shouting a variation on the same question. Decontamination? Why? What's going on?"

Terrance Schumer looked a short, ginger woman right in her eyes. He remembered the day she'd crossed the wall. The day she'd stepped inside. Got her number. Got her shots. Got her assignments, just like the rest of her fellow refugees.

He saw the snot running down her face. The bloodshot look in her eyes.

He felt guilt.

He felt regret.

Because he knew the truth. He'd known it all along, and he'd kept it from her. He'd kept it from his people.

"The fuck's goin' on here?" someone screamed.

Terrance Schumer glanced at Luis.

Then back at the crowd.

And he said the words he'd been dreading all morning.

All week.

All... ever.

"The virus is airborne. And some of us are carriers."

CHAPTER TWENTY-TWO

"You ready?"

"Not really."

"Good. On three. Two. One..."

Hayden held his breath as he barged through the metal rear door of the ASDA supermarket. It'd taken a full morning and afternoon of walking to find their first sign of life—or life as it used to be. Fortunately for them, it just so happened to be a shop. A shop the group had scouted for ages. Watched from afar. Kept a close eye on.

It *looked* derelict. *Looked* empty.

Hayden hoped to whoever was up there that was the case.

"Come on," Miriam called, waving the other thirteen group members along. They hadn't spoken much. Not since the incident at the cabin. Not since Bob turning. Since Rajiv, Bhvishya, all of them turning.

Turning out of the blue.

Out of nowhere.

"You going first or am I gonna have to brave it?"

Hayden looked at Miriam. She glared at him from beside the open door. Seemed quiet in there. Dust floated out. A good sign.

If dust had the chance to settle, it was usually an indication that people hadn't.

They didn't want to face any people. Not right now.

Not ever again.

Hayden walked in through the door. Stopping off at a supermarket wasn't ideal. But the truth was, they were hungry. Low on food. Low on water. Low on everything. If they were lucky, maybe they'd find a few cans of beans in this place. Or some tinned tuna. Anything tinned would do.

Oh, biscuits too. Biscuits didn't go off. If the rats hadn't got to them, they'd be a handy find.

Hayden walked slowly through the dark storage room of the supermarket. The stuffiness outside was contrasted by the coolness in here. Hayden heard nothing but the chatter of his group. Nothing but the squeaking of his own footsteps against the dirty tiles. Nothing but the thumping of his heart.

He reached the door at the back of the storage room. There was nothing in here. Already raided, evidently. Didn't bode well for the rest of the supermarket.

But they had to try.

Try, or starve.

He knew which he preferred.

"You look better when you're taking a bit of responsibility," Miriam said.

Hayden held the handle of the door leading towards the main supermarket area. He turned. Looked at Miriam. "What do you…"

"Stepping up to the plate. Leading. Like this. It suits you."

Hayden wasn't sure what to say to Miriam. He didn't want to lead. Didn't like the idea of leading anyone. Because he knew the chaos his leadership skills caused. He knew the loss that emerged whenever he got involved.

But he was at the front of the line. He was the one holding the door.

So maybe that's just how it had to be.

Maybe he was the leader Miriam wanted for her group. That the group wanted.

He turned back to the door, not saying a word in reply to Miriam, and gripped the handle tight. Listened to the silence beyond.

Lower the handle, investigate, get out of here.

Lower it, investigate, get out.

He thought about walking away. About running away. The thought crossed his mind way more than had to be healthy.

But he knew there was no way out. Not now. Not anymore.

Not now he was with this group. Really with them.

Not now they were with him.

So he lowered the handle.

Pushed the door aside.

Lifted the sharp metal pipe.

The first thing that hit Hayden was the smell.

"Oh, Jesus," Russell—one of the group members—muttered. "Is that dead?"

Hayden covered his nostrils. Looked around the empty supermarket. The lights were all out, of course, which gave these shops a really eerie hue. Something strange about a supermarket with the lights out. Something ghostly.

"It's something dead alright," Hayden said, stepping into the supermarket. "But I don't think it's zombies."

He walked past the rotting fruit and vegetables, which flies buzzed around, maggots swarmed. Most of the loose veg had been eaten away, but the veg in bags were blackened, little holes in the plastic where rats and mice nibbled their way inside, giving the flies an entry route.

"Least the vermin are keeping healthy," a ginger woman called Jill muttered. Always followed everything with a nervous little laugh. This included.

Hayden kept his hand over his mouth as he made his way

towards the canned food aisles. Miriam followed closely behind. As he scanned his surroundings—the broken glass lining the tiles, stale beer festering from smashed bottles, cheery mascots on children's cereal boxes grinning back at him like all was normal—Hayden couldn't help but cast his mind back to Bob again. Something happened. Something made him turn.

He remembered Little Tim. The way he'd turned out of the blue.

Just like Bob.

Just like the others.

"Holy shit. Rice fucking pudding!"

Hayden watched Jill run towards the rice pudding, almost slipping on spilled food. The air was sweet with decay. And although Hayden was relieved to find this place—although everyone seemed happy to finally have some food—he couldn't shake the feeling of wanting to get out of here. Wanting to get away.

Because something wasn't right.

He felt a nudge on his left arm. Turned, saw Miriam smiling.

She didn't say anything to him. Just kept on smiling. Blue eyes twinkling.

"What?" Hayden asked.

Miriam nodded at the group.

When Hayden looked at them, he saw them smiling too. Saw them laughing. Like their troubles, their travelling, all of it had been nothing, all of it was forgotten, all the loss and the pain was irrelevant now they had something to smile about, something to distract themselves with.

"You did good," Miriam said.

Hayden scratched the back of his neck. "I didn't really—"

"What happened to you? Before we met. Really."

Hayden's jaw tightened. His cheeks heated up. He remembered everything, right from the start. The fear and confusion he'd felt in the first days. The way he'd stepped up because he had to.

Then the loss that just kept on stacking up.

He found himself looking into Miriam's eyes and wanting to tell her everything. Wanting to open up. Because in a sense, he figured it'd make him feel better. It'd free him, somehow.

Instead, all he could say was, "I grew up too fast in this world. Now it's catching up with me."

He wasn't sure where those words came from. But he saw Miriam's eyes narrowing in concentration.

She put a hand on his arm. Offered a sad smile.

And in a soothing tone, she said, "You aren't alone there. Things will work out. For both of us."

Hayden felt Miriam's hand on his arm. Felt himself falling into her eyes. Heart racing. Laughter, joy, all of his present distractions slipping away into the background.

And the past, too.

Slipping away.

Becoming irrelevant.

Because he did have something to fight for.

People to fight for.

Someone to fight for.

He was about to tell Miriam more about his past when he saw the little boy watching from the back of the supermarket.

CHAPTER TWENTY-THREE

"Hayden? What is it?"

Miriam's words blended into the background of Hayden's consciousness. All sounds blended into the background of Hayden's consciousness.

All he could focus on was the boy at the back of the supermarket.

Standing there.

Staring at him.

He looked at the boy. Dark hair. Short. Skinny. Manchester United shirt dangling loosely over his tiny frame.

But more than anything, it was the look in the boy's eyes that Hayden saw. The fear. The fear of... something.

Not to mention the blood rolling down his cheeks.

Just like the boy Hayden let down.

Just like the boy he'd ran away from.

Hayden took a step in the boy's direction. He felt Miriam grab his arm, but it didn't feel nice anymore. It didn't feel soothing. Didn't feel anything.

"Hayden, what's—"

"That boy. There's a boy. He needs... he needs help."

"What boy?" Russell muttered. "There ain't a boy there."

Hayden kept on walking. A lump swelled in his throat. "There is. He's…"

When he stepped a little closer, he saw the boy wasn't there anymore.

The boy was gone.

Hayden stood there. Goose pimples rising on his arms. The taste of sweat covering his lips.

He'd seen a boy. Seen a kid.

Not a hallucination.

Couldn't be a hallucination.

Couldn't…

"Hey."

Miriam's fingers touched his arm again. Snapped him out of his trance. Behind, the rest of the group looked on with puzzled eyes.

Hayden looked into Miriam's eyes. Was he crazy? Was he imagining things again? Maybe he was. Maybe that's all this was. The boy was a figment of his imagination. An invention of his mind. A construct of his…

Then he heard the scream.

There was no denying it this time. Not with the way Miriam turned. Not with the way the rest of the group looked at one another.

A scream.

A child's scream.

A boy's scream.

"What do you think… hey! Hayden!"

Hayden didn't stick around to talk this one out.

He ran in the direction he'd seen the boy.

He ran to where he swore he'd seen him.

He had to be there.

He couldn't let him down.

Couldn't let another kid down.

Couldn't turn his back on anyone else.

He slipped over some spilled wine. Flies buzzed up from the crystallised alcohol. He ran out of the alcohol aisle, down past the meat, which rotted away, the smell even worse than the decaying veg.

It should've made him hurl. Should've made him puke his guts up.

But it didn't.

It just kept him running.

He heard Miriam call for him. Heard the rest of the group running after him. And he felt some guilt for leaving them behind. Some guilt for running away.

But he wasn't running away for self-interest. He wasn't running away to save himself.

He was running *towards* someone who needed saving.

Someone who needed his help.

Help that he should've given long ago.

He saw the double doors to his left swinging lightly. Ran through them, metal pipe in hand. He didn't know what awaited on the other side of this door. Didn't know how much he'd need the pipe. Just that the boy screamed. Which meant the boy was in danger.

Which meant he needed Hayden's help.

Hayden ran through the door. Barged through them into another storage area. This was just as gloomy as the last though it wasn't as dusty. Wasn't as empty. Boxes of electronics stacked on top of one another. A broken television lying cracked in the middle of the floor. A sign that looters had once been here. Barged in here to find anything of value to sell on in the new world.

Just a pity nothing had value anymore.

Nothing but food.

Nothing but life.

Hayden stopped in the middle of the dusty storage room.

Took a few deep breaths, tried to calm himself down. If the kid was in here, he needed to know where exactly. It was a maze of cabinets, of shelves, of makeshift wooden corridors and forklift trucks.

He needed to use his ears.

He needed to listen.

He needed to...

He saw something. Saw movement over to his left. Clear plastic twitching. Something behind it. Someone behind it.

Hayden crept up towards the clear plastic. Held the pipe tightly. If anyone were in here—anyone who tried to hurt his group, that boy, his people—then he'd kill them. He wouldn't hesitate. He couldn't, not anymore.

Hesitation was for the weak.

He wasn't weak.

He couldn't be weak.

He walked slowly towards the clear plastic. Saw it moving some more. Definitely someone behind it. Definitely someone waiting.

The boy? He wasn't sure.

Someone else? He didn't even like to consider that.

As he reached the clear plastic, every muscle in his body tense, he put a hand to it. Grabbed it. Readied himself to pull it aside.

Then, something dawned on him.

He'd been in this storage area some time now and nobody had come storming through the door after him.

No Miriam.

No nobody.

He pulled aside the clear plastic.

The little boy crouched there. Curled up in a ball. Only... no. It wasn't the little boy he'd seen before. This one was taller. Bulkier. Paler. Wearing a purple cardigan.

Hayden stared at him, stared into his chestnut eyes. The boy stared back at him.

"What..."

Hayden heard something click behind him.

He turned around.

Saw a man standing there. Bald. Wearing white dungarees. Narrow cheekbones. Fluffy beard that looked like it couldn't buy a fucking bristle. Piercing grey eyes.

"You come away from my boy and we can get this over with nice 'n quick," the man said.

He was holding a Stanley knife.

Pressing it to the first young boy's neck.

CHAPTER TWENTY-FOUR

"You come away from my boy and you step right over here. Step right over here like—like a man."

Hayden stared into the wide eyes of the bald man. He saw they were bloodshot. Feral. Like a rabid dog. An animal left neglected. Alone for way too long.

He pressed the unfurled Stanley knife into the young boy's neck. The one with the blood down his face that Hayden had seen earlier. So he was real. He was real, and he was in here.

He looked at Hayden with tearful eyes.

Hayden saw the desperation on his face clearly.

A bang at the door. Fists thumping against it.

"Hayden!" a muffled voice called. Miriam. But even though she was just through the door, she sounded so far away. So distant. Like this room was locked away from everywhere else.

Probably because it was.

"Your friends aren't gettin' in here," the man said. "Not—not until you bring 'um in here anyway. Soundproof. Did soundproofin' before the world went shitty. Did a good job, right? Did a good job, didn't I?"

Hayden saw the guy's eyes lighten up. Like he'd forgotten

where he was, what the situation was, for a moment. Hayden noticed just how much the guy reeked of piss. Combined with that rabid look in his eyes, he knew he was dealing with someone not quite sane. Someone with a distorted sense of reality.

The most dangerous kind of person.

"Just... just lower the knife from the boy's neck—"

"Don't fuckin' tell me what to do with my boy. Ain't that right, boy? He don't tell Daddy what to do. Say it!"

The boy whimpered. Cried. "He... he doesn't tell Daddy what to do."

The man smiled. Nodded. A smidgen of colour invaded his pale cheeks. "Right. Ain't that right. No one tells Daddy what to do. Not anymore."

Hayden stared at the man. His heart raced. There had to be something in here. Some way of getting around the man. Some way of fighting him.

The metal pipe in his hand.

Could he swing it at the guy? Swing it at him before the man slit the boy's throat?

The image of that unfolding filled Hayden's mind.

The little boy he'd let down.

The way blood spurted out of his neck; painted the glass.

The nightmares Hayden had been cursed with ever since.

He couldn't let this boy face the same fate. Not now.

Hayden lowered his metal pipe. The man watched him intently, narrowing those wayward eyes.

"I'm putting my weapon down. I'm going to walk away from your boy back here." Hayden pointed back at the boy hiding behind the clear plastic. "I'm going to walk out of here."

Hayden started to walk away from his weapon. Towards the left of the man, the boy. Could he grab the boy? Grab him and make a run for it? And what about the other kid?

He heard the banging at the door. Heard Miriam, Seb, the

other group members all shouting out for him. He could do with them in here right now. He could do with their help.

He didn't have that luxury.

He kept on walking towards the door. Away from the boy behind the plastic. Closer to the man with the Stanley knife. The man watched him closely. Kept the blade to the kid's neck. Would he slice? Would he have it in him to slice?

Hayden didn't want to find out.

"You—you brought people here. To take my boys. To take 'em away."

Hayden shook his head. "I came here with friends to find food. To find shelter. Not to hurt you or anyone."

"That's what they all say," the man said, growing twitchier, eyelids quivering. "Always say they ain't gonna hurt nobody. Always say everyone's gonna be fine. Everyone's gonna be okay. But they never are. No one's ever okay."

Hayden stared into this man's eyes. He saw tears building up in them now. Saw them growing more bloodshot.

"We're okay. I swear—"

The man shook his head. Slapped the side of his face. "No. No. No one's okay. Just me. Just me and my boys. All that matters. Can't have anyone else. Can't have anyone else 'cause anyone and everyone else always just goes away. Always just goes away."

Hayden felt the weight of the man's words. Aside from the fact he had a blade on the boy's neck—a way of playing on his emotions to get him away—he heard what the man said loud and clear.

He heard the distrust in the man's voice.

The distrust of others.

The lack of confidence.

The lack of faith.

All this man cared about was survival. His own survival. Not his boy's survival. If he cared about his boy's survival, he wouldn't have a blade to his neck.

He cared about himself.

Just like Hayden had before he'd met Miriam's group.

Hayden stepped up to the man. Slowly. Didn't want to risk anything. Didn't want to risk him cutting his boy's neck. Not after all this time. He ignored the rattling against the door. Ignored the sobs from the other boy.

He just focused on the man.

"I was like you once. Scared. Afraid of other people."

"Don't go poisonin' me with those words."

"I was afraid of everything. Everything new. I was afraid of stepping up. Being somebody. Just like you need to be. For your children. For yourself."

The man shook his head. Tears fell freely down his face now, hit the tiled floor below. "Words don't mean nothin'. Words don't mean nothin' at all."

"I'm walking away. But I want you to come with us."

"No! I don't. We don't. We're together. We're—"

"If you don't come with us, you're going to die in here. When your food runs out. When your water runs out. And I don't just mean your sons. I mean you, too. You're going to die in here because you didn't show the balls you need to survive in this world. You didn't show the leadership to make the tough decisions."

The man shook his head some more. The Stanley knife grew shaky on the boy's neck. He sobbed. Hayden saw the top of his scalp was all patchy, all flaky like he was losing his hair through stress.

"Hey. I'm sorry. For coming in here. For... for ruining what you have. For frightening you. But I swear. I swear to you, if you come with us, we'll keep you safe. We'll keep all of you safe."

The man glanced up. Wiped the tears from his eyes. Blood trickled from a skin-deep wound on the boy's neck. Terror in his eyes.

"Really?" the man asked. "You—you really mean that? For me? For me and... and for my boys?"

Hayden smiled. Nodded. "Sure. Just lower the knife."

The man and Hayden exchanged a long stare. Probably a lot shorter than it felt, in truth.

But eventually, the man lowered his Stanley knife.

Put it by the side of his son's feet.

"I'm just afraid. Just afraid of what'll happen. Just afraid of—"

The man didn't finish speaking.

Hayden booted him in his face.

Knocked him away from his boy.

Before the man could fight back, struggle free, Hayden grabbed the Stanley knife.

Straddled the man onto the ground.

"You put yourself before your boys. You put your own fucking pathetic self before the ones you're supposed to protect."

He lifted the Stanley knife.

Pressed it to the man's neck.

"Some people get a second chance. Some people deserve a second chance. Not you."

The man's eyes widened.

Hayden sliced his throat.

He felt the man's warm blood cover his hands. Listened to him gasping, spluttering like a pig. He heard the boys crying somewhere behind.

But as he crouched there, blood spurting out of the man's jugular, Hayden didn't feel a shred of guilt.

He'd done this to protect those boys.

He'd done this to protect his people.

Because that's what they were. His people. The ones he cared about.

He'd do it again in a heartbeat.

He waited for the man to stop twitching and gasping before stepping away.

Put the bloodied Stanley knife into his back pocket.

Walked over, grabbed the metal pipe.

When he turned, he saw the boys holding one another by the door.

Hayden walked over to them. Saw them cowering. Saw the fear building in their eyes. Smelled urine. Faeces. Horrible conditions they'd been put in. Horrible conditions they'd been forced to live in.

He looked back at the man, lying in a puddle of his own blood.

Then he looked back at the boys.

"You coming?" he asked.

The boys looked at one another. Looked at one another with tear-soaked faces.

Then, they nodded.

As Hayden opened the door back into the supermarket, he saw the boy he'd left behind clearly in his mind.

He saw him smiling.

He saw him saying thank you.

But the pride didn't last for long.

Not when he stepped out into the supermarket.

Heard the cry.

CHAPTER TWENTY-FIVE

Hayden should've known escaping the supermarket wouldn't be quite so simple as it sounded.

But watching Emily, one of the group, rip the guts out of Jill wasn't exactly what he'd expected to walk out to.

He stared out of the storage room. Emily was perched over Jill. Blood dripped down from her teeth; blood that Hayden could smell in the air, fresh and metallic.

Jill, bless her, was still alive. Still screaming. Still struggling.

Still fighting as Emily tucked in. Her face was completely pale but for the splash of blood that covered it, like spray paint on canvas.

Hayden stood, the two young kids by his side. Stood and stared as Emily ripped out Jill's intestines with her long, sharp nails.

Jill kept on screaming. Kept on crying.

A few seconds later, Hayden heard running. Heard the sound of contact, like something heavy crashing into something else.

When he looked to his right, he saw exactly what it was.

Miriam was fighting a zombie. Smacking it on the side of its head with a cricket bat she'd evidently found lying around in this place.

Only it wasn't just any old zombie.

It was Russell.

Russell had turned, too.

"I'm—I'm scared," one of the boys muttered. The skinnier one in the Manchester United shirt.

Hayden looked down at him. Put a hand on his shoulder. He flinched at first. Looked at him with fear in his eyes. Like a lifetime of fear had been building up inside them.

"You don't have to worry about a thing," Hayden said.

When he looked up, he realised he might be wrong about that.

Emily's zombie was standing. Tubes of intestines dangling from her bloodied lips. As the sound of fighting, shouting and groaning echoed around the derelict supermarket, Hayden watched as Emily stumbled towards him.

Jill had finally stopped screaming.

Which meant she'd be soon to turn.

Hayden stepped in front of the boys, the sour taste of fresh death filling the air. Not rot. It took time for a body to rot. But just a scent of difference. A hint of death to the air. Sweet. Sickly. Only way of describing it.

Hayden lifted the sharp metal pipe.

Waited for Emily to approach. The two boys closely behind him.

He watched as Emily picked up her pace. She stumbled, and her ankle split, the bone jutting out of her skin. Didn't bother her, though. Nothing bothered her.

All that bothered her was getting to Hayden.

All that bothered her was meat.

Hayden pulled back the metal pipe and rammed it into Emily's throat.

He pushed back. Pushed towards the top of her neck. Wanted

to take her down as quickly and confidently as he could. Didn't want to watch her wallow in this state of limbo for long.

But Emily wasn't stopping.

She kept on pushing.

Pushing against the pipe.

Pushing right against it, even though the sharp edge of the pipe was scraping her spine.

She kept on coming until Hayden realised he was going to have to let go.

"Quick!" he shouted to the boys.

Let go of his pipe.

Grabbed the boys' hands.

Ran, just as Emily tumbled forward, the pipe slicing right through her neck.

When Hayden looked back, he saw Emily still wriggling around on the floor.

Jill's eyes opened, and she started to rise.

Hayden ran past a few aisles. Kept his hands wrapped tightly around the boys' hands. He reached Miriam, who'd just about taken down Russell. Pinned him down under one of the shelves.

But Russell was still gasping, growling.

Even though his neck was covered in cuts and piercings.

"How'd it happen?" Hayden asked.

Miriam put her hands on her knees. Panted. "It—it just—they just turned. One sec, all's okay. Then they just—"

"Turned," Hayden said, nodding.

Miriam shook her head. Her eyes were narrowed, staring blankly at the floor. "I just... I just don't get how—"

She didn't finish her sentence.

Jill stumbled around the back of the shelves.

Lunged for the four of them.

Hayden felt the pressure on the boy in the purple cardigan's arm as he tried to run away. The boy cried out. Screamed.

No.

Hayden wasn't going to let him die.

He wasn't going to lose him.

He wasn't going to give up on somebody else. Not after all this time.

So he ran around the back of the boy.

Punched Jill square in her face.

Punched and punched until she fell back, all bloodied, skin still warm from when life ran through her veins.

He punched until she let go of the boy.

"What now?" Miriam asked.

Hayden listened to the shouts. Listened to the groans. The footsteps. Smelled that sweet scent of death growing in the air.

"We run," Hayden said.

The four of them ran down the shopping aisle. The main entrance was up ahead. They could try unlocking it from inside now they knew there was nobody around. Well, at least they hoped nobody else was around.

"How many turned?" Hayden asked.

Miriam shook her head, still panting. "I... I don't know. I was just... they were just..."

"It's okay," Hayden said.

"It's not fucking okay. Not at all."

"Well, maybe it's not okay. But we're here. We're here. And we're going to get out of this place. All of us."

They reached the end of the aisle. Looked to the left. A couple, Jacob and Neela, sat together. Jacob gripped his ankle, winced. They backed off, holding onto a sideward turned shopping trolley. The only thing they could put between them and the oncoming dead.

"We can't just leave them," Miriam said.

And although Hayden wanted to disagree, although he wanted to argue, he couldn't.

"No," he said. "No we can't."

He looked around at the boys. Looked them both in their

tired, distraught little eyes. "Miriam here's going to look after you. I'll be back for both of you. I promise."

Miriam frowned. "Hayden, what—"

"There's no other way," Hayden said. "We can't just leave them. Like you said."

"But I didn't mean—"

"I can handle myself," Hayden said.

Miriam didn't say another word.

She just shook her head. Looked away from Hayden.

Hayden took a deep breath and ran towards Jacob and Neela.

As he ran, he wasn't sure what exactly he was trying to do. Five zombies surrounded Jacob and Neela. All of them he recognised as old group members. And the fact he saw no source of the outbreak made him think about Little Tim again. Little Tim, Bob.

The virus.

It was changing.

Adapting.

Adapting in the most terrifying way.

"Jacob!" Hayden shouted. "Neela!"

They glanced up. Raised their eyebrows. "Hayden. We—we—"

"Neela, I need you to run out. Distract the zombies. So I can get Jacob away safely."

Neela shook her head as the five zombies closed in, pressed up against the shopping trolley. They hadn't noticed Hayden yet. But they would, soon.

As would many others.

Something he had to accept.

Something that might just kill him.

"Neela!" Hayden shouted. "You need to step out. You need to make a run for it. Please. Both of you. Your lives depend on it."

Neela curled herself up into a ball as the zombies kept on pressing against the trolley, pushing them further back into the wall. "I—I can't."

"You can."

"I'm scared."

"We're all fucking scared. But you just have to..."

It happened in an instant.

The metal of the trolley split away.

The zombies forced their faces through the crack.

They chomped down on Neela's face while still pressing against the trolley, still desperate to get closer to their prey.

Hayden watched as Jacob's face pressed up to the trolley.

As the metal forced through his skin, turned him purple, crushed him slowly.

He watched Neela and Jacob struggle to escape. Struggle to break free. But the more they struggled, the more the zombies fought back. The more flesh they sunk their teeth into. The more blood they spilled.

Hayden turned away as Jacob's skull cracked, crushed by the force of the undead.

He smelled fresh death in the air. Tasted that sweetness. The sweetness that would soon turn sour; that signified another loss of life. Another loss of hope.

He turned away from Jacob and Neela, knowing he could do nothing else for them, and looked back at Miriam and the boys.

When he saw the puddle of blood underneath them, a sudden coldness hit his core.

CHAPTER TWENTY-SIX

Hayden stared into the muddy hole in the back of the garden.

He held the gun loosely in his right hand.

Looked down as the rain fell, the night warm, the darkness thick.

He knew what he'd done.

He knew he'd had to do it.

But it would haunt him for the rest of his life.

THE SIX SURVIVORS made their way down a long country road away from the supermarket. Hayden, Miriam, the two boys, as well as two other people they'd bumped into on their way out—Renee and Anthony. They'd found a few bullets for Miriam's pistol back at a derelict house a few miles back, which was something. Old guy there had shot himself in the head, left a little gift behind. The night crept up on them like a predator, silent and watchful. None of them spoke. Not about events at the supermarket. Not about when to stop. Not about anything.

But Hayden knew from the silence that they were all thinking about the same things.

As visibility diminished, silence surrounding them but for their footsteps, the occasional cough, Hayden thought about the outbreak at the supermarket. The sudden outbreak amongst their own people. Amongst people he'd spoken to not much earlier. People he'd been with, been around, just moments before he stepped through that door to the storeroom at the back of the supermarket.

And then they'd turned.

All of them, turned.

Well, not all of them. He wasn't sure how many exactly. But a number of them had and then gone on to attack the people who hadn't turned.

Which meant one thing.

The virus was airborne.

Little Tim's turning back at Riversford confirmed that long ago. He was just too afraid to face up to it.

"We should rest," Anthony said.

Hayden squinted ahead. Saw a few detached houses lining the road. He knew they were getting closer to the wall. The zombies were building up in number. Made sense that any kind of wall guarding life would attract the dead like a magnet.

But Hayden and the group just diverted around them. Did everything they could not to bump into them.

They couldn't take anymore.

They couldn't put the two boys through anymore.

They'd found out the names of the two kids. Charlie and Sam. Charlie in the United shirt, Sam in the purple jumper. Turned out the man Hayden put down with a Stanley knife wasn't their dad at all, but a weird neighbour who always used to insist on giving the children a lift to places they wanted to go. Sounded to Hayden like he'd taken advantage of the apocalypse. Used it to his own benefit.

What mattered was that Charlie and Sam were safe now.

They were looked after now.

Properly.

"We'll take one of the houses on the right," Miriam said. "Search it bottom to top. Camp out upstairs until dawn breaks. Then we'll make our final push."

"In separate rooms," Renee interrupted.

"What?"

"In separate rooms. We... It'd be best if we camped out in separate rooms. Right?"

She looked around at Hayden. At the others. All of them understood. But it was just unspoken. Like speaking it aloud confirmed the truth, verified the new reality.

Sleeping in separate rooms meant that if any of them turned, they couldn't harm anyone else.

Every sneeze or sniff was met with inquisitive glances. The paranoia tired Hayden out. Part of him wanted just to go back to his old life. His life of looking out for himself and no one else. His life of no responsibilities. Of no ties.

But he knew that was bullshit now.

There was no going back.

Only forward.

Only onwards.

When they reached the first of the detached houses, they scanned the downstairs first. Took out a zombified old woman in the living room. Buried her outside in the garden with jumpers and shirts over their faces, just in case there was anything contagious.

They cleaned up the room where the woman had been as best they could. Couldn't get rid of the rotting stench though. Could never get rid of the rotting stench.

Hayden volunteered to sleep in the lounge. To keep an eye on downstairs.

Nobody argued against him.

They decided to get to sleep right away. Didn't say much to one another. Told the boys not to worry. That everything was going to be okay. That they'd be moving on to a better place tomorrow.

"Will it have people there?" Charlie asked.

Hayden smiled. Nodded. "Yeah. It'll have people there."

"Will it have children there?"

Hayden swallowed a lump in his throat. Rubbed a hand against his arm. "Yeah. Yeah, it will."

Charlie's eyes lit up. Just briefly, like all that mattered in the world right now was new children to play with.

Then he walked out of the lounge, towards the stairs.

Hayden saw Miriam looking through the banisters at him as Charlie past. And when he saw that hard stare, the reality of what he had to do flooded his mind once more, made the taste of vomit fill his mouth.

"Charlie," he said.

Charlie stopped. Turned. Looked at Hayden with his cute little eyes. His innocent, pale face. "What?"

Hayden felt weakness building in his muscles. "Just... just come to the garden with me a sec. There's something I have to show you out there."

He saw the frown on Charlie's forehead. The puzzled expression. "What... what is it?"

"It's a surprise," Hayden said.

Charlie stood still for a moment. The rest of the house was silent. Dark. Ready and waiting.

Charlie smiled. Walked back down the stairs. "Is it an adventure?"

"A kind of adventure," Hayden said, leading Charlie out of the lounge, towards the garden. "You just close your eyes and hold my hand."

Hayden grabbed Charlie's hand.

Eased him down the corridor.

Past the staircase.

Towards the kitchen, towards the back door.

He felt Miriam's eyes burning into his back with every step he took.

He thought he heard her sobbing.

When they stepped out into the pitch black garden, Hayden led Charlie down the steps, across the long, uncut grass, right to the trees at the bottom end.

"It's like Jurassic Park!" Charlie said.

Hayden wiped a tear from his cheek. "Yeah. Yeah, it is."

"You sound sad. Why are you sad?"

"I—I'm not sad. I'm happy. Happy we're all here. All of us. That we made it this far."

"And then we're going to go to the wall with the people and the children, aren't we?"

Hayden stopped. He couldn't reply to Charlie. Couldn't say a word. Tears rolled down his cheeks. His eyes stung.

"Hayden? Why are you crying?"

Hayden looked down and saw Charlie staring up at him.

His body went cold when he looked into Charlie's eyes.

But his body went even colder when he saw Charlie's arm.

The bandage wrapped around his left arm.

The blood staining through the dressing.

"We're going to be okay, aren't we Hayden?"

"Of course we are," Hayden said, smiling. He crouched opposite Charlie. Took both his hands. "Of course we are. You're a good kid. You're such a good kid."

"You're a good leader."

"I'm not a leader."

"You saved me from Nasty Nick! You're a good guy. He's a bad guy."

Hayden nodded. Wiped his eyes once more. Smiled. Smiled for Charlie more than anything. "You're one of the good guys, too." His muscles tightened. He couldn't do this. He wasn't strong enough. Didn't have it in him.

"I hope I stay with you forever."

"Me too. Me too."

Charlie smiled.

Turned around, looked at the tall oak trees at the bottom of the garden. Cool rain trickled down lightly from the dark sky above.

"Where's the surprise?"

Hayden pulled the gun out of his back pocket.

Held his breath.

Looked away.

"Hayden, where's my—"

The sound of the gunfire rattled through Hayden's body. Made it go cold. And as he listened to the echo, he hoped maybe this was a dream. A nightmare. Just like the other nightmares he had.

He prayed when he opened his eyes he'd be inside that house.

Or back at the shopping centre.

Or somewhere, anywhere but here.

Anywhere before Charlie got bitten.

Anywhere before this mess.

But then he heard a thud.

Heard Charlie's body hit the ground.

Silence.

HAYDEN STARED into the muddy hole in the back of the garden.

He held the gun loosely in his right hand.

The shovel in his left hand.

He looked down as the rain fell, the night warm, the darkness thick.

He knew what he'd done.

He knew he'd had to do it.

Because he couldn't let Charlie turn. Not because he was a threat. Not for any bullshit reason like that.

But because he was a kid.

He was a kid. He didn't deserve to come back as one of them. He didn't deserve to die a painful death. He didn't deserve the bastardisation of his life that the infection would cause.

But as Hayden stared down at the ground, dripping with rain, he knew what he'd done would haunt him for the rest of his life.

He turned round.

Walked back up the garden.

Looked upstairs.

Miriam stood by the window.

Tears rolled down her cheeks.

She nodded at Hayden, and Hayden nodded back.

Little Charlie was finally at peace.

CHAPTER TWENTY-SEVEN

Hayden and the four other remaining group members departed for the wall the following morning.

It was peaceful. Cool but bright. And as they approached an old town, seemingly derelict from afar, Hayden couldn't deny today just felt like a normal late spring day. A precursor to summer.

And then he remembered what he'd done last night and the taste of sick filled his throat.

He looked up at the apartment blocks either side. Looked at the boarded up windows. The smashed glass. This place was dead. Just not the kind of dead they were trying to avoid, fortunately_.

Well. Not that they knew of.

The town was laced with a stench of old litter. Anthony and Renee walked together, a little further ahead of Hayden, Miriam, Sam. Sam asked questions every now and then. Questions about Charlie. About what'd happened. About what was going on.

Hayden wanted to answer Sam. He tried to answer Sam.

But he couldn't get the sound of the gunfire out of his mind.

He couldn't get the memory of lifting Charlie's lukewarm body into the grave at the back of the garden out of his head.

"You okay?"

Hayden looked to his left. Saw Miriam staring at him. That expression of wide-eyed concern. An expression he'd seen far too many times in life for his liking.

Hayden nodded. Turned back to the road ahead. "Not seen any zombies for some time. Can't complain."

"I'm not talking about the zombies, Hayden."

Heat rose behind Hayden's eyes. "I know you're not. But I don't want to speak about—"

"You're going to have to speak about it at some point."

"No I don't!"

The shout surprised Hayden himself. Renee and Anthony turned around. Sam glanced up at Hayden and Miriam, fear in his eyes.

"Everything alright back there?" Renee called.

Miriam stared at Hayden. Eyes watery.

Then she swallowed a lump in her throat and nodded. "Yeah. We're just fine. Thanks."

Hayden watched Miriam walk ahead of him. Walk away, Sam's hand in hers. He knew he'd done wrong. He knew he'd been a fucking idiot to shout at her. Because she cared about him. She was concerned about him. That's all it was. Concern.

"I'm sorry," Hayden said.

Miriam stopped. Turned around. Nodded. "Like you said. You don't have to talk about it. Not if you don't want to."

Hayden opened his mouth to call Miriam back. Because he was wrong. He did want to talk about it. Okay, maybe not *want*, but he definitely needed to talk about it.

He couldn't let it eat away at him.

Couldn't let it build up inside.

Couldn't let guilt gnaw away at his conscience once again.

He was about to call Miriam's name when he saw the truck creeping up the hill towards town.

"Company," Anthony said, clearly seeing what Hayden saw. "Hide in one of the buildings or something?"

Hayden walked up and joined the rest of the group. Something about the truck seemed familiar. And yet it also seemed out of place.

"That's... that's one of the Salvation trucks," Miriam said. "Like the one that took me when I got close."

The truth crashed down on Hayden heavily. "But Salvation fell. Didn't it?"

Miriam stared ahead. Forehead wrinkling. "I don't know. I really don't know. But we have to hide."

They ran across the street. Tried six, seven doors before finally finding their way into the reception area of a hotel. The truck's engine rumbled on, grew closer.

Hayden and the others crouched beneath a window. Watched the truck creep along. It slowed down as it moved through the town. Inside, Hayden saw three people. The back door locked. People being taken, no doubt about that. Just like Miriam said. Approaching the wall, and then someone taking them on a long journey north towards the Salvation camp.

The man in the passenger seat glanced out of his window.

Looked Hayden right in the eye.

Hayden stayed still. Completely still. He'd seen him. He'd seen him and he was going to stop.

Hayden was going to have to fight back.

He was going to have to...

The man looked away.

The truck carried on its journey.

Hayden and the group perched in silence for a few minutes, maybe longer. Listened to the truck ease away from the town. To the right, filling in the silence the truck had left behind, Hayden heard gasps. Groans.

"Infected," he said.

Renee tutted. Rolled her eyes. "Just when I finally thought we were getting a modicum of peace."

They stepped out of the reception area. Looked at the zombies in the distance. Not many of them. Six. Seven. A few errant stragglers.

Nothing they couldn't deal with.

Hayden took down the woman with the greying, crumbling skin. Smashed the metal pipe right across her neck, pierced it through her throat.

He watched her stop moving the moment the pipe split through her neck. Watched her go still. The incident at the supermarket yesterday must've just been coincidence. The zombies that wouldn't die. The dead that wouldn't give in, no matter how much their necks were split.

The rules hadn't changed.

Everything was okay.

Everything was—

"Hayden!"

Hayden heard Miriam's voice. Heard the panic in it.

But when he turned round to face her, he didn't see zombies swarming her.

The zombies were on the road, completely still.

Miriam stood at the top of a hill on the road. She looked out at something. Smiling.

She pointed.

Hayden walked towards her. Then he started jogging. What had she seen? What had she seen that was worth smiling about? What had she...

He saw it.

He saw it, and the breath left his lungs.

In the distance, at the bottom of the hill, there was a wall.

A long barbed wire wall stretching on for miles. As far as the eye could see. Cutting right through the middle of roads, like it'd just been constructed wherever possible—or like it'd sprouted up from the ground.

He couldn't see beyond the wall, but he didn't have to.

He saw masses of people surrounding it.

Swarming towards one area in particular—a tunnel.

People.

People just like him.

Just like Miriam.

"We made it," Anthony said, grabbing Renee and holding her tightly. "We flipping made it!"

Hayden listened to the laughter, saw the smiles.

He stared into the distance.

Stared at the wall.

"Not yet," he said.

CHAPTER TWENTY-EIGHT

Katrina Holt held her breath as she squeezed into the dark confines of the tunnel.

It was morning, but in the darkness of this tunnel, it was impossible to tell that much. It was cool outside, dry, but not Katrina. Not her two bambinos, Walt and Harry. Not anyone in the mass of refugees trying to reach the other side of the tunnel. Trying to reach safety. Everyone was damp. Covered in sweat. Just the new normal. Just the way they felt. Just what they had to deal with.

Sounds of chatter and excitement surrounded her, packed into this tunnel like sardines, forced to move forward. Couldn't turn back even if they wanted to.

But why would they want to?

Why would anyone want to?

"Mummy, I can't breathe proper."

Katrina looked down at Harry. He clung onto her hand. The tears on his face told her straight up exactly what he thought about this tunnel, about the situation they were in. Walt was a lot better. Little bit older, aged twelve. Harry was still only seven.

And he always had been a more difficult child. More sensitive. Jamil used to say he'd cry at the wind if it pushed him over.

Katrina smiled at the memory of Jamil. Sweet, friendly Jamil.

She hoped he forgave her for what she'd had to do to him.

They moved further down this long tunnel. Katrina had no idea how long it stretched on. The walls looked pretty flimsy from outside, but she could see on her way in that the tunnel led right across to the other side of the city. A way of working out what to do with an oncoming mass in plenty of time. Smart, really. Clever.

She just hoped the rumours weren't true.

As she held her boys' hands tighter, tried to keep her footing in the ever increasing pace of the crowd, she remembered what Sol told her back in Wolverhampton. Something about a partition. About this place being too full. About the guards here turning people away.

And she'd seen the trucks. Seen the trucks filled with people. Driving them away from the wall, taking them somewhere else.

She didn't want that. She didn't want to be thrown in the back of a smelly, cramped truck with her children, taken to some unknown camp in the middle of nowhere.

She wanted this.

She wanted her freedom.

She deserved her freedom, didn't she?

"Mummy, I feel really sick," Harry said.

"God," Walt groaned. "Does he ever stop complaining?"

"Walter, don't speak to your brother like that."

"But he's—"

"Hey, young man. Might not have school anymore but I'm still your mother. Do as you're told."

Walt tutted. Shook his head. Loosened his grip on Katrina's hand.

"It's okay, young man," Katrina said, leaning into Harry's ear. "We'll be all okay soon. All of us."

"Will Dad be here?"

A lump swelled in Katrina's throat.

"Of course he won't," Walt said.

"Walter."

"What? It's about time he realised Dad's d—"

Katrina did something she'd never done in her entire life.

She smacked Walter across the face.

Walter grabbed his cheek. Looked at his hand. Then looked back at Katrina in shock, surprise.

She didn't know what to say to him. Didn't know whether to apologise or what. She'd never smacked him or any of her children before.

But speaking about Jamil was out of line.

Upsetting his younger brother was way over the mark.

"Grow up," Katrina said, choosing not to apologise for what she'd done. "Be a man. Not a boy. A boy acts immature. Says hurtful stuff to his family. A man loves his family. You're the older brother now. Be the man."

Walt looked like he was about to bite back with some venomous bile.

And then a sound screeched through the tunnel.

The crowd slowed. Katrina lost her footing.

The sound. It came from ahead. It came from...

Shit.

She saw the light peeking through the end of the tunnel. Saw the city beyond. The buildings. The place where she could live. Where she could raise her children.

"They letting us in?" someone behind her asked.

"They frigging better be," someone responded.

They waited. Waited, as footsteps echoed at the end of the tunnel. On tiptoes, Katrina could see people. See people dressed in black gear.

Holding guns.

Wearing...

"What's that racket about?"

It took Katrina a few moments to realise what the noise was. The crying. The shouting. The sound of things being thrown, of metal being rattled.

And then she saw people behind the wall in the distance.

People, all dressed up nicely, all washed and trimmed.

Angry people.

Throwing stones towards them.

Holding placards: *Keep Infected Out Of Our Border! We're Full! GO HOME!!!!*

Katrina stared at the angry mob of people. She stared at them in a state of shock, much like many of the other people around her. This place was supposed to be kind. This place was supposed to let people in.

She saw a few people at the front of the group run towards the guards.

"Back away," someone called. "Turn around. You'll require full authentication, full decontamination, before entering."

Full decontamination? What did that mean?

"Mummy, I'm scared."

Katrina rubbed her fingers through Harry's hair. "Don't be scared, bambino. Don't be scared one bit. They're just people. Just worried people."

"But why are they worried about us?"

Katrina pondered Harry's question.

Why were they worried about them?

And then the gunfire snapped her out of her trance.

She watched the refugees sprinting towards the guards fall to the ground.

Watched blood splatter from their heads.

Watched bullets fire into the crowd.

Pandemonium erupted. Screams filled the tunnel. Some ran one direction; others ran the other.

More gunshots.

More blood.

More panic.

Katrina tried to run away, but she fell.

She fell, and as she did, she dragged her boys down with her.

Felt feet trample over her.

Smelly boots stamp on her face, crack her bones.

She clung to her boys' hands as the chaos erupted. As the panic continued. And as her consciousness slipped away, she told herself everything was going to be fine, everything was going to be okay. This was just a hitch. They were just worried. They were just paranoid.

She was still holding her sons' hands when the door at the back of the tunnel closed.

When darkness filled the cavern.

She was still holding her sons' hands when she woke up.

Woke up in a large sports hall type area.

Confused. Disoriented. Mouth dry, dehydrated.

"What..."

She was still holding her sons' hands when the gas sprayed out of the ceiling.

The yellow, greenish gas fell on them.

When the burning filled her throat.

Crippled her lungs.

She fell forward. Held onto Harry. Held onto Walt. She tried to tell them everything was going to be okay as their eyes streamed. As blood rolled down their nostrils. As they cried, coughed, wailed.

She tried to tell them everything was okay as she burned from the inside out.

But she knew it wasn't.

Finally, she knew it wasn't.

The next time she drifted into unconsciousness, it was an unconsciousness she'd never wake up from.

Terrance Schumer stared out of his top storey window at the wall. The numbers diminished around it. A few stray people allowed inside. Just for show. Just to give the residents a false illusion that everything was okay. That some people had been "decontaminated". That the truth—the undeniable truth—was nothing more than a conspiracy.

He heard a knock on his door. Turned around, saw Luis standing there, eyes steely, sweat rolling down his forehead.

"Well?" Terrance asked.

"It's done," Luis said.

Terrance nodded. Looked back at the window. Back at his beautiful city.

He wiped a tear from his eye and hoped God would forgive him for his sins.

CHAPTER TWENTY-NINE

The longer Hayden and the group walked, the further away the wall seemed to get.

Morning stretched on to early afternoon. The sun hid behind the clouds now, giving a welcome coolness to the air. They walked down a long road, an old dual carriageway of sorts. Either side of them, grassy embankments. They had no way of knowing what waited for them either side. What watched them.

Hayden wasn't sure he wanted to know.

He just had to get to the wall. Get to the wall.

They all did.

The road was suspicious by its absence of cars. Its absence of life, or death. It was like an unused film set. Or a closed stretch of a road.

It'd been cleared. Which added fuel to the fire that where they were going was populated. Where they were going welcomed people like him. His group.

Or maybe that was just wishful thinking.

"Don't you find it weird that there's no signs?" Anthony asked.

Miriam frowned. "What d'you mean by signs?"

"Well, first thing I'd do if I were trying to welcome people aboard Boat Anthony is put a few signs up. Freedom This Way! That sorta thing."

"Maybe they're worried about the kind of people they'll attract, Miriam said.

"Or," Renee cut in, "perhaps they are averse to attracting anyone at all."

Hayden wasn't sure where he stood on the wall. Just that he had to get to it. He had to see what was behind it for himself. There were some things that bothered him. Many things. The truck driving through the town a few miles back. A similar truck to the one that took him to Salvation. To that prison.

He was starting to wonder if the same people were driving those trucks that lived behind the wall.

He just didn't know why.

Yet.

"Least none of us have turned yet," Anthony said, grin on his face. "But if you start sniffing anytime soon, do us all a favour and keep your distance, yeah?

"Same applies for you," Renee said. Then a pause. "Do you really think the virus is airborne now?"

Hayden saw Renee turn to him. Saw everyone turn to him. He wasn't sure why. But he'd been the one to come up with the theory in the first place, so perhaps it was something to do with that. "We can't be sure. But signs suggest—"

"The injections," Renee said. "The ones they gave us back at Salvation. Perhaps they had something to do with it?"

Hayden thought back to Little Tim. He hadn't been injected. He'd wondered about the injections himself at first, especially after the state of Bob's arm. But he was okay. The rest of the group here were okay. And Little Tim turned bite-free long before jabs were being doled out. "I'm not sure. I don't think so. But..."

He stopped when he saw the movement at the top of the embankment on the left.

"Ah, shit," Miriam said. "And we were doing so well."

Six zombies stumbled down the side of the grass. Hayden could smell their rot, see flies buzzing around them from here. So they were old ones. Ones that'd been out here a while; infected some time ago.

"Sam, you go over to Anthony and Renee. We'll deal with these."

Sam ran over to Anthony and Renee, who turned away from the oncoming zombies. The numbers were increasing. The groans were becoming a chorus, a chant.

Hayden stepped up beside Miriam. He held the sharp metal pipe. Miriam held a gun in one hand, a cricket bat in the other.

"Ready?" Hayden asked.

Miriam nodded. "Ready."

They ran towards the first of the zombies like it was just procedure. Like it was just routine. Hayden swung the pipe at the skull of an old man, his skin so grey and wrinkled he looked like he'd been sat in a bath for weeks.

Hayden watched his skin split away as he pounded the metal into his head. He lowered it. Pressed it up against his already-bitten neck.

Pushed the spike right through it.

He had a flashback to the supermarket. The zombies that wouldn't die no matter how much he messed up their necks. And as he pushed the sharp edge of the pole into this old man's neck, Hayden saw the increasing mass of zombies and knew they wouldn't stand a chance if they didn't fall. They'd have to run.

Then the man's body went limp and he tumbled to the ground.

His head dangling on loosely by rotting flesh.

Hayden wiped his forehead. Breathed a sigh of relief. One down... a good few to go.

But they were falling.

They were falling, so they were manageable.

They were falling, so—

He felt a hand grab his left ankle as he lunged forward.

Turned around.

The old man was clinging onto him.

Teeth snapping.

Staring up at Hayden, his head barely hanging on.

"Shit," Hayden muttered. He turned. Saw the growing mass of zombies coming towards them. Surrounding Miriam. Surrounding Renee, Anthony. Sam.

"They're—they're not dying!" Miriam shouted. She fired three bullets into the neck of a lanky ginger guy launching itself at her.

It fell to the road beside her.

Went still for a moment.

Then its teeth started snapping and it pushed itself up again.

Hayden looked around. Looked at the zombies pouring over the embankment. Too many to deal with if they did fall, but definitely too fucking many to deal with when they didn't fall.

"What do we do?" Anthony shouted.

Hayden swallowed a lump in his throat.

Gripped onto the metal pipe.

"We run," he shouted.

Nobody needed any encouragement.

They all ran as fast as they could down the road, towards the wall. Zombies kept on appearing at the top of the embankment as if from nowhere. He saw a man with half his face ripped off, maggots chewing away. He saw fresher bodies. The body of a Hispanic looking woman, two young boys beside her. Where were they coming from? Why the fuck hadn't he seen them earlier?

"Over the next embankment," Anthony called.

Miriam shook her head, panting as she ran. "But we don't know what's—"

"We have to try!"

They kept on running. Hayden heard the echoing groans behind them. The droning cries. His feet were sore, blistered. His mouth was dry. They couldn't fail now. Not now they were so close to the wall. Not now they were so close to getting behind it. To finding out what was hiding within.

But then he heard someone cry out.

Looked over his shoulder.

Anthony was crouched on the road. His ankle was twisted at an impossible right angle.

He looked down, pale-faced with horror.

Behind him, the mass of undead poured down the road.

"We... we can't go back," Miriam said. "We need to keep moving."

Hayden thought about Miriam's words.

Then he thought again about everyone he'd lost.

Everyone he'd let down.

"Hayden, we can't—"

"I'm not letting anyone else die," he said.

And then he ran away from Miriam and Sam, back towards Anthony.

When he got there, he crouched beside Anthony.

Renee was tearful, hysterical, constantly looking up at the approaching zombies. "He—he just toppled over. Just keeled over."

"You go," Anthony said, shaking his head, wincing with pain.

Hayden put a hand on Anthony's shoulder. Shook his head. Did everything he could to keep the zombies out of his view, out of his mind. "We're not leaving you behind."

"You have to. Or they'll get us all. They'll—"

"So be it," Hayden said.

Anthony looked him right in his eyes. And for the first time, Hayden got the sense that these people really respected him.

That they believed he was being sincere.

That he wanted to help them.

Lead them.

He wrapped his arm around Anthony's back. Started to lift him up, Renee doing her best to grab his other side.

"Just try not to walk on that ankle, mate," Hayden said.

"Easier said than—agh!"

Anthony squealed with pain as his foot made contact with the road.

"Come on," Hayden said. "One step at a time. One step at a time."

He could hear the zombies behind getting closer.

Noisier.

Smell them closing in.

In the distance, he saw Miriam and Sam waiting. He saw the road ahead. The road to the fence. To the wall. To freedom.

The final steps.

They kept on moving, the zombies so close to nipping at their heels, just metres behind.

But they could do this.

They could make it.

They could…

Then, Hayden saw the truck.

Speeding up the road.

Speeding towards Miriam and Sam.

Towards them.

"Is that…"

Anthony didn't finish his question.

His words blurred away in Hayden's mind.

The truck was exactly the same as the one he'd been bundled into and taken to Salvation.

The same as the one the people had driven, taken him away to that prison.

Speeding from the fences.

Speeding towards his group.

CHAPTER THIRTY

Hayden froze as the truck sped towards his group, as the zombies closed in behind him.

He heard Renee shouting something at him. Heard Anthony calling out. And up ahead, he saw Miriam standing by Sam's side. Waving. Waving at Hayden to join her. For the group to join her.

But all he could focus on was that truck.

Even though the zombies were inching closer, all he could think about was that truck.

Coming from the wall.

The same people, as he'd suspected all along.

Coming here to take them away from this place after travelling so, so far.

He looked over his shoulder. Looked back at the rotting mass of zombies edging ever closer.

And then he eased Anthony to his feet once more.

"You're gonna have to run," he said.

Before Anthony could protest, Hayden started running.

He felt Anthony grip onto his right shoulder. Felt him dragging him down. On Anthony's other side, Renee held on, trying to keep her husband upright. Anthony screamed as his twisted—probably broken—ankle hit the road. He screamed so loud that Hayden's ear started ringing. He grew certain that he was going deaf in that ear sometime soon.

But he had to press on.

He had to keep on moving.

Keep on fighting.

Miriam had already missed out once before. She'd already made this journey and had it cut short. Not again. Not again.

She didn't deserve that.

Hayden ran towards the truck. Saw it pulling up. He watched as a man in a black outfit climbed out. He waved at Miriam, at Sam. Then at Hayden, Anthony, Renee.

Miriam just stood still.

Stood still and stared as the man tried to bargain with her.

Hayden couldn't hear him through the growling mass of the monsters.

He didn't have to.

He knew what the guy's game was.

He knew exactly what was happening here.

He watched as Miriam shook her head. But he could see the man had a gun. If she didn't at least try and blend in, he'd shoot her. He'd shoot all of them. He had no doubts about that. Not now.

Not after he'd seen the guards butcher the prisoners back at Salvation.

Killing wasn't the ideal option. But if it were necessary, it'd happen.

As Hayden ran, clinging on to Anthony, he started to wonder why the people behind the wall would do this. Why they'd send out trucks to take people away. To deter them from crossing. To lock them away far, far away. But then he realised. All of a sudden, he realised. The world had always been this way. Whenever people needed help—weaker people—the strong always turned them away. It happened in the Middle East. It happened all over the world. People fleeing conflicts. The world pretending to give a shit.

But not enough of a shit to let those people into their homes, to share their food, their shelter.

Well that was changing.

Right now, that was changing.

"Quick!" Hayden heard one of the men shout. "Get on board or they'll have you. They'll have you any fucking second."

Hayden stopped beside Miriam. Beside Sam. Two men were outside the truck now. Both staring at the group. Both holding guns.

"We just want to go to the wall," Miriam said.

"We'll take you some place safe."

"Like Salvation?" Miriam shouted. "Like—like one of your other prisons?"

The main guard's beady eyes narrowed. "You're one of the Salvation escapees?"

"I'm a fucking human being. And I'll tell you right now I'd rather die out here than step in that truck with you. I'd rather take my fucking chances out here than inside that truck. Not again. Not after all we've gone through to get here."

The men looked at one another, engine of the truck still rumbling.

Then they looked back at Miriam. Hayden. The rest of the group.

"Very well," the guard on the right said.

He lifted his gun.

Hayden heard the gunshot. But he didn't process what was happening. Not completely.

All he knew was he felt blood splash onto his face.

Then he heard more gunfire. Gunfire from Miriam as she took out her pistol, fired back.

He ran towards the guard still perched in the driver's seat. Threw himself inside.

The guard pointed the gun at him. Glasses steamed up. Fear on his face.

"Don't make me shoot you," the guard said. "P-please. Don't make me shoot you."

Hayden looked through the grill at the back of the driver's cabin.

He didn't have to see in the darkness to know that tons more people were packed in there.

He turned back to the driver.

Slammed the gun from his hand with the metal pipe.

Then he stabbed him in the throat.

Hayden pushed the driver away. Sent him tumbling down to the road below. The keys. The keys were still in the engine. They could use this vehicle. To get to the wall. To get to the other side.

He leaned out the window. "Quick!"

The guards were dead. Lying on the road.

But the zombies were here.

Miriam fought off a greying old woman. Renee pulled her husband along, Sam by their side.

"Shit," Hayden muttered. Wasn't a driver. Never passed his fucking test. But the new world had taught him a thing or two about practical experience.

He started to accelerate. Stalled the vehicle. Started it up again, driving towards the mass of zombies.

He swung the truck around. Crunched a few bones in the process.

Pulled up right by Miriam, Renee, Anthony, Sam.

"Quick!" Hayden called.

He watched the group run towards the truck. Grabbed Sam's hand, lifted him up. Helped Miriam up. Took Anthony's hand, lifted him, and then Renee's.

When they were all inside the truck, Hayden slammed the

door. Split a zombie's flailing hand in two in the process. And as he sat there, rain peppering down from a storm cloud above, the sound of zombies muffled outside, he couldn't help but feel proud. Because they'd done it. They'd fought off the guards. They'd taken this truck.

"We can press on towards…"

His elation subsided when he saw Anthony clutching his stomach.

His bleeding stomach.

His gunshot stomach.

CHAPTER THIRTY-ONE

"Hold in there, Anthony. You hold in there."

Hayden gripped the wheel of the truck and drove down the empty, stretching road. The zombies were but dots in the mirror now, far, far away. Nobody seemed to pull him up for his driving abilities, so he figured it didn't make sense to mention that he couldn't legally drive.

That was the old world.

This was the new world.

All rules, all regulations, were different now.

"Don't you worry sweetheart," Renee said, holding Anthony's hand as he bled out from the gunshot wound in his stomach. "We'll get you safe soon. We'll get you safe."

"You sure this is the best route?" Miriam asked, leaning towards Hayden.

"Do you know a better route?"

"I don't mean it like that. I just—"

"All that matters right now is getting to that wall. I don't know how long it'll take whoever sent this truck to realise we've taken out its crew. I dunno what they'll do if and when they do find out.

But that doesn't matter right now. All that matters is we get there. We get to safety."

"And the people in the back?"

Hayden glanced in his rear-view mirror. Saw the movement in the back of the truck. He smelled them, too. The refugees. Because that's what they were—people just doing all they could to escape a conflict-stricken region to reach somewhere safer.

Just like Hayden.

Just like Miriam.

Just like everyone.

"We spoke to them," Hayden said. "They understand the score. They want safety too. And this might be their best chance."

"But if something goes wrong?" Miriam asked.

Hayden glanced away from the road. Looked Miriam in the eye. "Things have been going wrong since way before the apocalypse broke out. We've made it this far. We can make it a little further."

He offered a reassuring smile to Miriam.

Didn't feel all that confident about his words. Didn't feel any sort of profundity in what he was saying.

But Miriam's eyes softened. She smiled back.

Must've worked.

Must've—

"Stop!"

Hayden swung around when he heard Renee's shout.

He saw the dog on the road. And it startled him. A golden Labrador retriever. His favourite kind of dog. Used to have one when he was a kid. Called it Charlie. Went everywhere it went.

Charlie died not long before Hayden's older sister Annabelle died.

No wonder he'd ended up as fucked up as he had.

He saw the dog in the middle of the road. Skinny. Bony. Blood dripping down from its messy muzzle.

Swung the truck to the right.

Only the truck didn't turn as expected.

It spun. Spun sharply to the right. The tires screeched against the road. The vehicle started to topple. Screams erupted from the refugees in the back of the truck.

"Hold on!" Hayden shouted.

He wasn't sure if anyone heard him.

The truck slammed against the road.

All the glass inside shattered, some of it raining down on him, nicking at his face.

As Hayden lay there, disoriented, head spinning, he thought he was in silence. That everyone was dead. Everything was over. He wasn't sure if he'd blacked out. Sure felt like someone had hit the reset button on his consciousness.

He wasn't sure about anything.

Then he realised it wasn't silent at all. His ears were just ringing so loudly they were covering up his sense of hearing.

But Hayden heard loudly now.

He heard the pained cries.

Smelled the burning fuel.

The truck. The truck was on fire. The truck was fucking burning.

He looked to his left. Saw Miriam squinting, blood rolling down her sweaty head. To Miriam's left, Sam. Renee. Anthony. Anthony wasn't moving. Renee was crying. Sam looked stunned, like he couldn't be any more afraid than he already was.

Hayden reached over for Miriam. Grabbed her hand. Struggled, tried to help her out of the truck. It was burning in here, filling with smoke. If they didn't get out soon, they'd all choke to death. Every one of them.

Including the...

Shit.

The people in the back of the truck.

They'd gone silent.

Hayden pulled himself out of the truck, Miriam following

closely behind. The others climbed out too—Sam, Renee. They had to help Anthony out, though. And judging by his closed eyes, by the stillness of his body, the blood rolling down his forehead, there wasn't much to save of him.

Hayden jumped down by the side of the truck. Saw the scale of the damage. The road wobbling with the heat of the burning. Black smoke billowing out the engine.

"Gonna have to get moving," Miriam called, as Renee crouched on her knees, crying over her husband's still body.

"The people in the back—"

"It's gonna explode, Hayden. It's gonna explode, and if we don't get away, none of us are gonna make it."

Hayden walked around the back of the truck. Walked to the doors, which he knew would still be locked shut. "So be it."

He stepped in front of the doors.

And then he noticed something.

Noticed something in the distance, way ahead of the truck.

At first, he thought they were zombies. But they were running. Running away from Hayden, from the truck, from the group, who were surely easy prey right now.

Then he realised they weren't zombies at all.

"That's... That's them," Miriam muttered.

Hayden couldn't help but smile as he watched the refugees run towards the wall. Watched them sprint for their lives. He didn't know what lay ahead for them. Didn't know what fate they'd meet at that wall, on the other side.

But as he watched them run, watched the Labrador retriever sprinting behind them like this was all some kind of game, he felt proud.

Because he'd got them here.

Stopped them getting thrown into a hellhole like Salvation.

He'd given them another chance.

He heard Renee wailing and it snapped him out of his pride.

He looked at her. Looked at her perched over her husband's

body. A lump swelled in her throat. To come all this way then lose Anthony. It was harsh. Cruel.

He owed her some support.

He owed her that much.

Hayden started to walk over to Renee, away from the burning truck.

"Renee, I'm so sorry," Hayden said. "I'm sorry this had to happen to you. I'm sorry this had to…"

Then, something unexpected happened.

Anthony's eyes jolted open.

He shot upright.

Grabbed Renee's neck with his teeth.

Pressed down.

Ripped her throat out.

There was a moment's shock. A moment's complete silence, even from Renee, as her husband chewed away at her neck, as she choked on her blood, wide-eyed.

And then Anthony threw his wife back, smacked her head against the road, and ripped off her face with his teeth.

Then, Renee finally screamed.

CHAPTER THIRTY-TWO

Hayden watched Anthony rip his wife's face away and listened to her screams.

He couldn't do anything. Nothing but stare. Neither could Miriam, and it would've been cruel to expect Sam to do something.

Rain fell from the thick clouds above, breaking the stuffy air. The taste of blood lingered in Hayden's mouth. The smell of burning erupted from the crashed truck.

Renee continued to scream.

Hayden ran towards her, still unsure of what was going on. Anthony hadn't been bitten. He'd just turned. He'd been shot, and then the truck crashed, then he'd turned.

What did it mean?

How had he turned?

Why had he turned?

He stopped just opposite Anthony. Legs wobbling. Still unsure of what to do, of how to react.

Anthony looked up from his wife. Her torn-away nose dangled from his blood-soaked teeth. Renee was unrecognisable as she lay on the road, her face a mush of torn skin, of ripped-up flesh.

But still she edged from side to side.

Wailed.

Poor woman. Poor fucking woman.

Hayden watched Anthony rise to his feet. Instinctively lifted his right hand, then realised the metal pipe wasn't in there anymore. The Stanley knife was gone from his pocket, too.

Anthony continued to rise. Not a fraction of his old self in his eyes. Just bloodshot. Anger.

"The gun, Miriam," Hayden called. He held his right hand out.

Miriam just stared on blankly as Anthony edged towards him, as Renee finally went silent.

"Miriam, the gun!"

Miriam jolted. Reached for the gun.

Threw it at Hayden.

Hayden grabbed it.

Lifted it.

Pointed it at Anthony's face.

"Sorry, Anthony."

He pulled the trigger.

No bullets fired out.

Hayden looked back at the gun. Safety still on. Shit. Still not used to all this crap. Still not—

Anthony grabbed his right arm.

Grabbed it with immense strength.

Closed in on it, teeth clicking, eager for a bite.

Hayden started to pull back from Anthony. But he knew it was no use.

So he punched.

Punched at Anthony's face.

Punched at his neck.

Punched as hard as he could, gun in hand, bloodying Anthony's face even more than it already was.

He looked to his right. Saw Miriam holding Sam. Eyes wide.

Stunned. Startled. He wanted her help, but he knew how it was; how it felt. He'd been there before. Been frozen in shock.

He had to deal with this one alone.

Had to—

He saw Renee rise behind Anthony.

Saw her stand perfectly upright, the bones in her spine crunching as they twisted at an impossible angle.

Then, blood dripping down from the mess that was once her face, she walked towards Hayden.

He punched at Anthony again, doing all he could to dodge his snapping jaws. The desire to fight this battle himself drifted away. "Miriam, please! I need a hand!"

He felt Anthony pressing right into his chest.

Felt the blood from his mouth splashing against his body.

He was so close. So close to biting him. So close to pushing him over. So close to...

Hayden lost his footing.

Fell back on the road.

Anthony's weight on top of him.

He struggled against Anthony, who was inches from his neck now. But he had a grip on the gun. A good chance to remove the safety.

But doing so meant stopping pressing back against Anthony.

He held his breath.

Reached to remove the safety.

Anthony's teeth pressed against Hayden's chest.

Hayden put the gun to Anthony's head.

Pulled the trigger.

He heard the sound of the gunfire split his skull, make his ears ring even more.

He felt blood. Warm blood. Felt it cover him. Bathe him. Clog up all in his eyes.

He felt Anthony's weight fall onto him, crushing him even more.

And then he heard Renee gasping as she crept towards him.

Hayden looked up. Squinted through the clotted blood in his eyes, the taste of metal strong on his lips.

He pointed the gun at Renee.

She fell before he pulled the trigger.

Miriam slammed a large rock into what was left of Renee's head. It knocked her to the ground. But Miriam didn't stop there. She perched over Renee's body. Smacked the rock into her skull. Onto her neck. Slammed and slammed and slammed.

When Renee had gone quiet, when her head was nothing more than a pulp on the concrete, Miriam slammed the rock a few more times.

Then, she backed away. Blood smeared across her face. Silence filling the road.

Hayden pushed Anthony's body aside, which still twitched, fortunately mouthless and headless after the gunshot.

He stood. Walked over to Miriam. Put a hand on her shoulder.

"It's okay," Hayden said. "It's done now. It's done."

Miriam stayed on her knees. Stared down at the bloody pattern where Renee's head once rested. "I just... I don't understand. I don't understand how it happened. How he turned."

Hayden nodded. He walked over to Sam, who hid behind an abandoned car. He held out a hand to him. Half-smiled. "You okay?"

Sam glanced around at the dead bodies, fear in his tear-soaked eyes.

Then, after a few seconds, he nodded.

Took Hayden's hand.

They walked away from the truck. Away from the bodies. Miriam stood eventually. Joined them. The three of them. The only ones of their wider group left.

They stood in the middle of the road. Stood, hand in hand.

Stared ahead at the running mass of refugees who'd escaped the truck. At the Labrador chasing behind them.

"Shall we go?" Hayden asked.

Miriam swallowed a lump in her throat.

Then, she nodded.

Squeezed Hayden's hand.

Hayden looked back into the distance.

At the road ahead.

At the fences.

The wall.

They were getting there.

They were getting inside.

One way or another, this was ending. Today.

He walked down the road. Picked up a wrench from beside an abandoned car.

Then, together, they walked.

CHAPTER THIRTY-THREE

It was another hour before Hayden, Miriam and Sam reached the wall, and already, Hayden was having doubts.

The sun had burned through the clouds, making it a pleasant afternoon. Hayden's arms burned in the heat, hotter than any late springs he could remember in recent history. Maybe it was another thing the end of the world had prompted. Maybe there weren't just zombies, but fucked up weather patterns, too. He didn't know how this had all broken out. Probably never would. Who's to say it wasn't weather related?

Might seem far-fetched, but so too did a bunch of blood-thirsty undead trying to hunt him down. He lived in a world of farfetchedness. That was just life now.

He stared ahead at the long, empty road. The wall etched ever nearer. He didn't like how silent it was. Not just within his group —Miriam and Sam hadn't spoken a word for ages. But outside, too. Beyond his group. No groans of zombies. No shouts or cries of people. Nothing.

It seemed peculiar that a supposed boundary between old Britain and new Britain would be so... lifeless.

Hayden licked his dry lips. Didn't matter what he thought. Didn't matter whether he worried about it or not. Whatever was behind that wall would be there whether he gave a shit about it or not. All he could do was see for himself. Discover what secrets lay beyond.

He wasn't sure he was ready for it. Not after what happened with Anthony. With Renee. Not now the group were down to three. Another dwindling group. The whole reason he'd gone off the whole group dynamic in the first place. Groups collapsed. Groups decayed.

He didn't want to lose anyone else.

Didn't want to lose Miriam.

"She was pregnant, you know?"

Miriam's words came out of nowhere. Hayden turned to his left. Saw her staring at him as they walked further along the road. Her eyes were bloodshot, filled with tears.

"She found out back at the supermarket. Took a test. Confirmed it. She didn't want to tell Anthony. She was scared, I guess. Scared of what he'd say. Scared of the problems it'd put on the horizon. Scared of... scared of creating another problem in a world that didn't need any more damned problems."

She wiped her eyes. Shook her head.

"She was waiting to get to the wall. To tell him. He never knew. He—he ripped her face off and he never knew."

The image of Renee's face being violently torn away under the force of her husband's teeth was still fresh and prominent in Hayden's mind. He shook his head. Took a deep breath. "They were good people."

"They *were* good people."

"And we'll do what they wanted us to do. To honour them. We'll reach the wall."

"What if it's all bullshit?"

Hayden slowed. Frowned. "You're the one who wanted this place. More than anyone, you wanted this place."

"I did. You're right. But what if it really is just hell? What if it's fucking worse than it is out here? What if it's all for nothing?"

Hayden looked ahead. Looked at the fences. The wall. "I find it hard to believe anything can be worse than out here."

"You really believe that?"

Hayden nodded. "Yeah. Yeah, I do. Now come on. While we've still got some energy."

They walked for another thirty minutes, maybe longer. The continual silence built a sense of foreboding inside Hayden. The empty road. The empty patch in front of the wall. He swore when he looked down on it from afar that it'd been filled with people. Filled with life.

Something had happened here.

That's the only thing he was certain of.

"My legs are tired," Sam said.

"I know, kiddo," Hayden said. "I know. But we'll be there soon."

"Will Charlie be there?"

Images of the garden flashed into Hayden's mind. Holding the gun. Pulling the trigger. "No," Hayden said. "No he won't."

"Because he's dead?"

Hayden glanced over Sam's head at Miriam. Saw her wide, watery eyes. He thought about lying to Sam. Covering up the truth. Protecting his innocence, whatever.

But instead, he looked back down at him. Looked him right in the eye.

"Yeah. Because he's dead."

"Are we going to die?"

"I don't know."

He didn't like the brutal honesty with which he spoke. And from the shaking of Miriam's head, neither did she.

But that was just the state of affairs now.

Kids needed to know the truth. The next generation needed to understand what was at stake. To survive. To live.

"But I can promise you I'll do everything I can to make sure we don't," Hayden said.

Sam smiled at him. Nodded. Eyes so droopy, so tired.

Hayden smiled back at him.

The smile didn't last for long.

Not when he heard the voice crackle through the loudspeaker.

"Attention. Turn around. Border closed. Turn around and wait for further instruction."

Hayden squinted into the distance, towards the wall.

"Is that..." Miriam started.

Hayden saw the people in the distance. Saw them right in front of the wall. Saw them watching. One of them holding a loudspeaker.

All of them holding guns.

"I repeat. Turn around. Border closed. Turn around and wait for further instruction."

Miriam shook her head. "No. Not after coming this far. Not after—"

"If you do not comply, we will be forced to respond with due force. This is an infection-free border. Turn around and wait for instruction."

Hayden stared down at the wall. At the fences. At the tunnel leading through into the world beyond.

He stared at the men holding their guns.

A part of him wanted to comply.

To turn around.

To walk away.

But no. He hadn't walked this far to give up. Not now.

"Come on," he said.

He took Miriam and Sam's hands and started walking.

Hayden kept his head upright. Walked defiantly in the direction of the fences.

"Hayden, what if they—"

"They won't open fire."

"But what if they—"

"What else have we got?" Hayden shouted.

Miriam stared into his eyes.

Then she shook her head.

Tightened her grip on Hayden's hand.

Kept walking.

The voices didn't echo out of the loudspeaker for some time after. Or maybe it wasn't long at all. Maybe it just felt that way because with every footstep, Hayden became more aware of the guns pointing at him, of the words he'd heard.

Infection-free border

What did they mean by that?

What did they mean by any of it?

"Hayden, I don't like this."

"I don't. None of us like this. But it's what we have to do."

"Maybe we could come back when it's dark. Try—"

"We're not turning..."

Hayden's thoughts were interrupted when he saw the golden retriever at the bottom of the hill.

It was still. Covered in blood. Bony ribs on show. Tongue dangling out of its mouth.

Lying in front of it, masses of dead bodies.

People.

It didn't take Hayden long to realise who these people were.

"The people from the truck," Miriam muttered, coming to the same conclusion.

"I repeat once more," the voice said, louder now than ever before. "This is an infection-free zone. Stepping within the boundaries is a selfish act. A selfish act towards all the population living healthily within."

All the population living healthily within...

But what was the selfish act?

What was so selfish?

Miriam gasped when she saw the dead bodies. When the

truth dawned on her, invaded her. "We should turn back. We should go."

But Hayden wasn't being turned.

Not as the heat built up in his face.

Not as the tension twisted at his stomach.

He wasn't turning back.

He wasn't turning anywhere.

He was getting beyond that wall.

He was surviving this.

He was—

"As carriers of the virus, you are required to stay well away until further notice."

Hayden stopped. Didn't mean to. Just stopped, in the click of a finger.

Carriers of the virus.

Carriers of the virus.

And all of a sudden, it made sense. A twisted kind of sense.

Little Tim.

Bob.

Anthony.

All the people he'd been around.

All the people who'd turned.

Without bites.

Carriers of the virus.

"Step back slowly. This does not have to escalate."

But Hayden didn't process the words. Didn't take them in, not properly.

All he heard were the words spinning around his mind.

The truth overwhelming his thoughts.

You are a carrier.

CHAPTER THIRTY-FOUR

Hayden walked ahead of Miriam and Sam, away from the wall.

The sun was getting lower. A slight chill was building in the air, more reminiscent of winter rather than the late spring it actually was. But it didn't really affect Hayden. Not really. He was aware of it, but only in the back of his mind.

Because all he could think about was the wall.

All he could think about was the scene he'd discovered when he'd reached it. The dead bodies. The dead dog.

All he could think about was the words.

Carriers of the virus...

He looked ahead at the long road. It stretched into the distance; abandoned cars piled up in the middle, fields either side. The only sounds Hayden was aware of were footsteps; his own footsteps, the rest of his group's footsteps. Well. Hardly a group anymore. Not the best name for it.

The trio.

Because that's all that was left.

That's all that remained.

He felt a tightening in his stomach whenever the memory of

the wall guard's words entered his mind. Because it reminded him of everything that'd happened. All the people who had died around him. He'd suspected the virus was airborne. Suspected it for quite some time.

But a carrier...

Someone who carried the virus but didn't turn.

Why hadn't he considered that?

If that was true—which it was—then didn't the people behind the wall have a point?

They didn't want carriers amongst their masses. They didn't want the virus beyond their walls.

The expulsion of the few to save the many. It made sense. It added up.

"We heading anywhere in particular or are you just gonna mope all day?"

Hayden heard Miriam's words. She seemed... calm. Unaffected. Which he couldn't understand. She'd been the one to bring him here. She'd been so convinced that the wall was where they needed to be; the place they needed to reach to secure their safety. But she'd barely said a word. Just walked behind Hayden, holding little Sam's hand.

Sam was quiet. Wide-eyed. Confused.

"Hayden. I'm speaking to you."

"I guess we find some place to rest."

"So we're just giving up?"

Hayden shrugged. "I don't see what else we can do. You heard what he said. We're carriers."

"We don't know that's—"

"A little boy turned out of the blue a few weeks back. A little boy in a group of mine. No bites. Nothing like that. And then he passed it on to his mother. Again, no bites."

"That doesn't mean—"

"It adds up," Hayden said. "You might want to try denying it but you can't. It's the truth. I dunno about you, and I dunno about Sam but... but I'm a carrier. I'm a carrier, Miriam."

Hayden felt strange muttering the words. Brought a sour taste to his mouth. He was a carrier. That's who he was. That's what he'd become. That was his place in this world.

"So say you are a carrier. You're probably gonna want to try and get away from other people. Aren't you?"

Hayden swallowed a lump in his throat. Looked past Miriam, back down the road they'd walked along. "It'd be best if—"

"Just listen to yourself. Listen to yourself making excuses again."

"It's a valid excuse."

"It's a bullshit excuse. One you can hide behind to keep yourself away from other people. To shy away from responsibility. From leadership. Which is just what you've wanted all along really. Isn't it?"

Hayden shook his head. "That's not fair."

"This world isn't fucking fair. Nothing about it's 'fair'. 'Fair' went out the fucking window when people started chewing each other. When they stuck their teeth into other people's necks and spread a fucking monstrous virus."

Hayden glanced at Sam. He didn't seem fazed by Miriam's language. He supposed he'd heard and seen plenty worse since the world collapsed.

"So go on," Miriam said, holding Sam's hand. "Be honest with yourself. Be honest with us. Do you want to walk away? Do you want to be alone? Because remember, I gave you a choice. I gave you a choice back at the prison after you helped us. I gave you a choice at the barn. A choice that you took, then came on running back when it suited you."

"It wasn't like that."

"Do you want to be alone, Hayden? Because if it is, then you walk the fuck away. Because you're not safe to be with. Not because you're some 'carrier' or whatever bullshit they spouted behind the wall. But because you aren't *with* us. Not really."

Miriam's words echoed around Hayden's head. He met her watery eyes. Then Sam's wide eyes. His heart pounded. He had to be honest. He had to tell the truth. Open up.

He opened his mouth. Got ready to say the words.

I'm not coming with you.

It's better if we go our separate ways.

I'm trouble...

But instead, Hayden found himself closing his mouth. Licking his lips. Swallowing.

"I'm with you," he said.

"You what? Speak up a little."

"I'm with you."

He looked Miriam in her bloodshot eyes.

She nodded. "Good. You better be. Because we didn't lose our people for nothing. Anthony didn't get shot for nothing."

Hayden turned away. Started walking down the road again, still heading away from the wall. He wasn't sure where they were going. Wasn't sure what Miriam was planning.

Just that they couldn't give up on the wall.

It'd probably end up getting them killed, but they couldn't give up on it.

He took a few steps when a thought tightened its grip on his mind.

"Anthony didn't get shot for nothing."

He stopped. Heart picking up. Eyes narrowing. Not really looking *at* anything in particular. But thinking. Just thinking.

"Hayden?"

"Anthony didn't get shot for nothing..."

He remembered the way Anthony turned after getting shot.

The way he attacked his wife.

He remembered the way Bob turned.

Bob, who had the mark on his arm. The flared-up mark from the injection.

He remembered these two incidents and his head started to spin.

"Hayden? What's wrong?"

Little Tim. Where did Little Tim fall into the equation?

Fuck, did it matter?

All that mattered is what he realised.

All that mattered is what he now understood.

He turned around. Looked at Miriam, then at Sam.

"I think I know what's happening," Hayden said. "And I think I know how we can use it."

"Use... use what? For what?"

"To get inside the wall. To get to safety."

CHAPTER THIRTY-FIVE

Terrance Schumer stood outside the fences of the walls staring at the mess.

He didn't come out here often. Especially not at sunset. Didn't like the risk that came with it. But Luis and his advisers had been very specific and very demanding when they told him they needed him here tonight. That they wanted him to see the extents they'd had to go to in order to keep peace outside the walls, to keep peace within the walls.

And now, standing right here, he wished he hadn't bothered leaving the safe confines of his top storey apartment block at all.

The sun was low in the pinky, orange sky, but the scene in front of Terrance was clear. He could see the bodies. Still bodies of men. Of women. Of children. Of a dog, even. He could see the bloodied gunshot wounds in their heads. He could see the look in their eyes. The look of fading hope.

They must've known. They must've known what was happening to them as they approached the walls, the fences.

They must've known they were about to die right before it happened.

"Not what we wanted to do, sir. Wanted to keep it cleaner. But they found a weakness in the wall. Had to do what we had to do."

Terrance glanced to his left. A man called Daniel stood there, rifle in hand, white mask over his mouth muffling his speech. A white mask just like the one Terrance wore. Just in case. Just in case the airborne virus spread.

That's the line they were going with.

That's the approach they were taking.

Terrance looked back at the dead. His heart sunk every time he saw the little blonde girl holding her teddy bear, clinging it tightly. Because of all the people—all the sweat-soaked, urine-stenching people—she was the one who had the most hope in her eyes. Hope that she'd find refuge beyond the wall. Refuge beyond the fences.

Refuge in New Britain.

You let these people down. You failed them.

He nodded. Sighed. "You did what you had to do. Like you say."

Terrance turned around, back towards the long, dark tunnel.

"Sir, if you don't mind me asking. What're we going to do about inside?"

Terrance stopped. Looked back at Daniel. "What about inside?"

Luis lowered his head. Glanced back up at Terrance. "People. Citizens. They're... they're taking the crisis into their own hands. Forcing people—migrants—out of their homes. Killing them in the streets. I respect that we need to control the virus, especially if it's airborne and especially if migrants from outside are carrying it, but... but surely there's a better way?"

Terrance heard the screams from his city. His beautiful city. The scream of another migrant who'd found refuge there. A migrant who'd been willingly taken in. Taken in by a family with open arms.

Now stabbed to death.

Stabbed in the street.

Burned, to reduce the chance of the airborne virus spreading.

And Terrance felt a sense of guilt. Felt an immense sense of guilt for what events had come to. For the way in which the truth had forced his hand.

But ultimately, what mattered more than anything were the lives of the many.

What mattered were the lives of his people beyond the wall. They were the ones he'd sworn to protect.

And the numbers from outside were just overcrowding the place. Stuffing it with... well, undesirables. People who he hadn't been charged with protecting. People from outside. Foreigners, some of them feral, some of them too adapted to this horrible new world outside the fences.

"If you find a better way, tell me," Terrance said.

He walked back down the tunnel. Back towards his city.

"Until then, you... you keep the people aware. Keep them aware of the threat from outside. The threat from within as long as the migrants are amongst our people."

"Respectfully," Daniel said. "We—we haven't seen any evidence of airborne spread. Not within. Not yet."

Terrance stopped. Bitter taste in his mouth.

He looked back at Daniel. He'd pulled the white mask from his mouth now. Breathing the cool night air freely.

"No," Terrance said. "No, you're absolutely right."

He nodded at Luis, who stood behind Daniel.

Luis lifted a pistol.

Shot Daniel in the back.

Shot him three times.

Daniel's eyes widened. His skin went instantly pale. The remaining three guards looked on, horrified, bewildered, as Daniel fell to his knees.

"We haven't," Terrance Schumer said, walking over to Daniel, crouching over his spluttering body. "But we will. All of us will."

He felt a sense of regret building inside him once more.

Felt it intensifying as Daniel struggled on in the final moments of his existence.

He watched the dark blood drool out of the three bullet wounds on his back.

Waited.

"We'll all see it for ourselves. Very soon."

He put a hand on the back of Daniel's head.

Stroked it.

Then he stood up.

Walked back down the tunnel.

Back beyond the wall.

Back to security.

Behind, he heard the struggle as Luis ordered the other guards to lift Daniel's body.

He sensed the delayed panic. The confusion.

But he knew he'd done the right thing.

He knew he'd done what he had to do.

He was a leader. He was responsible for saving the many.

If that meant getting rid of the few to achieve his cause, so be it.

As the sun set, Terrance Schumer prepared for a long night.

But he knew the world would be a much better place the following morning.

He knew everyone would be much safer from the outsiders.

He knew he was doing the right thing for humanity.

CHAPTER THIRTY-SIX

Garth Cooley enjoyed his nights at the wheel way more than he should do.

He pressed his foot on the gas. Stared out at the darkness. There was something about the dark that eased him. Something that settled him. And he knew it was mad. Knew he was crazy for thinking that way. The dark was dangerous. Shit hid in the dark. He knew that. He was aware of that.

But there was something about *not* being able to see what was in the distance that calmed him, too. Something about driving down these abandoned roads, no light but the moon and the stars, his headlights, that made him feel alive again.

It took him back to his lorry runs. Damn them, he used to hate his lorry runs back in the old days.

But now, in this world, he realised how good he had it. How lucky he was being a member of the new society. The society behind the fences.

Just a pity his job was to round people up to escort away from their new world.

It was cool in the truck. Didn't turn the heater on though.

Didn't want to run the battery down. Not that the world was short of spare batteries—just he'd always been funny about wasting things. Food. Water. Old clothes. Always found a use for them. Always found a way to conserve them, right to the very end.

He glanced at his TAG watch. Remarkably, he hadn't looted it. One of the few items he'd held on to. Special to him. His daughter, Alison, bought it for him before she moved to Vietnam with that Asian chap, Kao. Gave up all her money, her top job at an insurance firm, everything, all to live some life in the middle of the Laos wilderness.

He didn't hear from her anymore. Obviously not anymore—nobody heard from anyone overseas. But he hadn't heard from her for five years before that point either.

He hoped to God she was okay. Hoped to God she'd stuck to the wilderness. Hoped to God Kao kept her happy, kept her safe.

He looked around the front seats of the truck. Empty. He was often alone these days. Not that he minded—he preferred being alone to spending hours in this shitty vehicle with a meathead, that was for sure.

But he couldn't help but long for some kind of connection. Some kind of truthful, *real* involvement with another human being.

He couldn't help but crave some normality.

He sniffed up. Caught a whiff of the minty air freshener, which was going off. Better smelling that than the sweat from the back. From the refugees he'd picked up. Terrance Schumer and the bulk of the people behind the fences preferred it if they were referred to as "migrants," but by Garth's definition, they were people fleeing war. People just looking for some safety. Just looking for a fresh start away from all this bullshit on the outside.

In the early days, there had been more leniency. There had been cases of helping the refugees beyond the fences. Smuggling them in. Hiding them in homes.

But gradually, those acts of kindness slipped away.

Reached bursting point.

And now that the news of the virus going airborne was common knowledge—the news that people on the outside with increased exposure were likely to be carriers—there was no room for sympathy or leniency, not anymore.

Garth kept on driving along the darkened road. He kept on looking for people. Signs of life. People he was tasked with taking away from the fences. Taking to one of the other stations set up across the country. A place within the chaos where they could be safe, happy.

Better for them that they didn't reach the fences. Not with the way the people within treated the people outside anymore.

A bitter taste filled his mouth as he flashed back to earlier that evening. A guard, Daniel. A guard he'd been good friends with. One of the decent ones. He'd walked back through the tunnel bleeding out from a gunshot. He'd been taken into the hospital area... and then he'd turned. Just turned, out of nowhere.

The bulk of the main city saw it. Saw him lunge at Doctor Parmer. Saw him rip away his throat.

All without a bite mark on Daniel's skin. All without being bitten.

Proof that the virus was airborne.

Proof that they needed to act against it.

Garth tightened his grip on the steering wheel. Accelerated further away from the wall, into the darkness.

He wasn't sure what was happening. Wasn't sure when it was all going to come to a head; when it was all going to end.

But he knew he just had to keep on doing his job.

Because he was helping people.

Helping people find a better life.

Helping them survive.

He saw a flash in the distance.

He put his foot on the brake. Slowed down. Heard the rubber tyres screeching against the tarmac.

He switched off his lights. Submerged in total blackness.

He'd seen something. Seen a flicker of light up ahead.

Something was out there. Something was waiting.

He stared at the spot where he'd seen the flash. All he could see was darkness. He didn't want to alarm whoever—whatever—it was. He'd turned his lights off to see whether it really was a light. A torch. A headlight. Whatever.

But nothing was there.

Nothing but darkness.

Garth rubbed at his stinging eyes. Maybe he was imagining things. Maybe he was just tired and needed some rest. He'd been awake since three a.m. A good solid twenty-one hours wide awake. Mind playing tricks on him. Eyes screwing with him like they so often had since he'd lost everything.

There was no flash.

Nothing in the road.

Nothing up ahead.

He looked back up into the darkness.

Took a deep breath, caught a whiff of his own sweat.

He flicked on the headlights.

Someone was standing there.

He couldn't believe it at first. Couldn't wrap his head around it. But there was no doubt. No denying it.

A little boy.

A little boy with curly brown hair and a purple cardigan.

Garth frowned. He muttered something to himself under his breath, but he wasn't sure what.

He pulled the handbrake. Grabbed the passenger door. Opened it up. What the hell was a little boy doing out here alone in the middle of the night? What the hell was...

When he landed on the road, he realised his mistake right away.

He felt something press into the back of his head.

Heard a click.

And then a woman's voice.

"Give me your keys and get in the back. Now."

CHAPTER THIRTY-SEVEN

Maya Harper thought she had a new family when the Jones' let her into their home.

She lay on the side of the road. Her head hurt. Her throat was sore. She could taste nothing but dirt and the metallic tang of blood on her lips. She didn't know what to do but lie there and cry. Didn't know what to think.

Just that she'd lived with the Jones' for weeks and they'd been so nice to her.

They'd taken her in when her mum and dad went away and made her feel welcome.

And now she was out here, in the streets, bleeding.

She lifted her aching neck. Looked at the empty streets. It was dark, but she knew there were people around. People around like her. Only the people like her—the ones who'd come from the other side—were mostly dead. They hadn't made it.

She knew she didn't have long left. Not out here. Not as one of *them*. Not as an outsider.

She'd heard the rumours. She was only thirteen, but she was old enough to understand the rumours. The rumours about the infection spreading. The rumours about it going from person to person without bites. But she didn't know what to think. She didn't know what to believe. Dan Jones told her she was infected so to get out his parents' home, but Maya didn't feel infected, so she wasn't sure about anything.

Only that Dan, the oldest of three Jones brothers, kicked her out the house.

Actually kicked her out.

Threw her into the road.

Told her to stay well away from his family. Not to come near ever again. 'Cause his mum was sick. His mum was sick and it was Maya's fault. All Maya's fault.

She expected one of the other family members to come out of the house. To come out to help her. Maybe Pete, the middle brother, who was always friendly with her, always wanted to joke around and laugh. Or maybe Mr Jones. He was serious, but he looked out for Maya. She knew he'd never hurt her. Knew he'd never abandon her.

But none of them came out the house.

None of them.

People just watched from behind their partly closed curtains at the events outside.

White masks covering their faces.

Fear in their eyes.

And Maya wondered what she'd done wrong to deserve this... this treatment.

She heard gunfire. Heard it up the road, up ahead. Looked up, neck still stiff, vision still blurred.

She saw a man holding a gun. A man in black. Wearing a thicker mask than the rest of the people.

He was firing bullets into the heads of the fallen people.

The fallen people like her.

And then a man beside him—a man dressed in a thick white outfit wearing scary goggles and an old World War style mask— shot flames out of a gun at the fallen bodies.

She watched the fire illuminate the darkness. Listened to the flames crackle. Smelled the charred, burning flesh drifting towards her.

She knew she had to get away.

She knew she had to hide.

But there was nowhere to get away to.

Nowhere to hide.

She tried to crawl along the road but her legs were sore, stiff, aching from where Dan Jones tripped her. She stuck her hands into the gravel. Dragged herself further along the road. The gunshots got louder. The smokiness from the burning bodies closer.

As they got closer, Maya couldn't help thinking back to the time she'd said goodbye to her mum and dad. To the burning smells then. The burning as the crashed car set on fire. The car that crashed as they tried to escape the zombies, as they tried to get away.

And Maya heard their screams in her mind, over and over again.

She saw her mum's pained eyes. The words on her lips. "Go, Maya. Run."

She remembered when the flames spread to Mum and Dad's bodies.

When the screams and the squeals kicked in.

She remembered crying, trying not to listen, doing everything she could to get away from the burning car, from the surrounding zombies as the screaming and crying carried on.

And then she remembered the last thing she heard.

The very last words her mum screamed.

"Please don't go Maya please help us please!"

Then another agonised scream.

Then, nothing.

She stuck her hand further into the ground. Pulled herself along. The gunshots and the flames so close now. And as they approached, it was those words that echoed in Maya's ears. The words that woke her from her nightmares. Her mum's last words.

"Please don't go Maya please help us please!"

The desperation in her voice.

The truth to her words.

She wanted Maya to be safe.

But she also didn't want to die in agony.

And she had.

She heard the footsteps stop right beside her.

She turned. Looked up at the two men. One of them holding a pistol. Another holding the flame-thrower.

She looked into the eyes of the man with the pistol. Saw a tear running down his cheek.

And then she looked at the windows of the houses. The twitching curtains. The terrified stares.

She saw a few of the people look her in the eye.

She knew they knew she was alive.

But they were too afraid to do anything about it.

Too afraid for their own family.

For themselves.

"I'm sorry," the man with the pistol muttered.

Maya opened her mouth to respond.

She didn't finish.

TERRANCE SCHUMER LOOKED down at the chaos on his streets and knocked back a Cobra beer.

"It'll be over soon, sir," Luis said. "All of it'll be over soon."

Terrance swallowed a swig of the bitter, flat-tasting Cobra. "I hope so, Luis. I hope so."

He caught a glimpse of himself in the mirror on the opposite side of the room.

The beard on his face.

The bloodshot eyes.

The monster he'd become.

All in the name of protecting this great new world.

All in the name of the future.

He gulped down some more Cobra and prayed for unconsciousness.

Hayden McCall watched the two vans disappear from the entrance to the fences; to the tunnel.

He watched as they headed towards their missing vehicle. Towards their colleague, "Garth," who hadn't reported in for over an hour. Disappeared off the grid.

He took a deep breath.

Turned around.

Faced the tunnel entrance.

Then, he stepped inside.

CHAPTER THIRTY-EIGHT

The darkness of the tunnel was thick, intense, almost tangible.

Hayden ran as quickly as he could through the tunnel. He wasn't sure how far he'd been running. He heard his footsteps echoing around, bouncing off the walls. Now and then, he swore he saw movement in the pitch black shadows. Someone watching. Readying to attack.

Didn't even matter if there was someone there. Not really.

All that mattered was he kept on running.

A stitch crippled at his stomach. The smells of the place were rich. Smells of people. Smells of a thousand stories. He hoped the people who'd broken into this tunnel—much like the people he'd ended up in the truck with on his way to Salvation—were okay. He hoped some of the ones who'd made it this far survived. That they hadn't been through hell at the hands of the people behind the fences.

Because he knew the truth now.

He knew the truth about the virus. About its spread.

He just needed to prove it.

Prove it, somehow, and... well. Hope.

He tasted sweat on his lips combining with bitterness. A bitter copper taste. Like blood. He knew what that meant. Something bad happened in here. Killing. Murder. He knew the taste from a mile away.

He just had to hope the guards at the wall were distracted trying to locate their "missing" truck long enough to get through this tunnel.

He just had to hope Miriam and Sam pulled through.

He kept on going through the tunnel. Became conscious of his racing heart, thumping at a similar speed to his echoing footsteps. Was he moving too fast? No. No, he had to move this fast. He had to keep on moving. He had to keep on going and going until…

A noise. A noise to his right. He looked up. Squinted in the darkness.

No sign of life. Nothing.

Realising he'd stopped, Hayden kept on moving through the tunnel, picking up his pace again. Truth be told, he was surprised how poor security was in this place. Either they were extremely distracted, or… something else.

Something else he didn't want to think about.

Something else he didn't want to ponder.

He ran further and further until he saw movement.

This time, he was sure of it. Up ahead. Someone moving towards him.

And then a voice.

Impossible to comprehend—too far away—but definitely a voice.

He stopped. Looked around. Looked for somewhere to hide. He couldn't fail. Not now.

So he threw himself to the right of the tunnel. Perched beside a kerb. Wasn't sheltered, wasn't disguised, but hopefully out of the way enough for whoever was approaching not to notice.

He waited there for a minute. Held his breath. The voices

grew louder. Footsteps closer. Sounded like they were jogging. Jogging towards him.

"...Just hold on."

"I can't—"

"You need to. You know we need to."

As Hayden curled up into more of a ball, he quickly became aware that these voices didn't sound threatening. They didn't sound dangerous or like the voices of guards.

They sounded terrified.

Like a terrified husband. A terrified wife.

Hayden waited a few more seconds. Held his breath, listening to the gasps of the oncoming people, the running people.

Were these people trying to get away?

What were they running from?

What was...

"Shit," the man said. "They're coming, Shelly. They're fucking coming."

"Hold it together, Paul. Hold it the fuck together."

"How am I supposed to—"

"Ssh!"

Hayden listened to the silence. The silence that fell in place of the sound of their running.

He strained. Tried to listen for a noise.

Who was coming?

What was coming?

What was...

Then, he heard the moan.

The moan came from his left. Not from the direction he'd been expecting. From the direction he'd come from.

He turned back. Looked in that direction.

He saw figures. Darkened silhouettes drifting towards him. Drifting towards the man called Paul, his wife—Hayden assumed—Shelly.

He saw them waddling closer.

Waddling out of the open gratings at the sides of the tunnel.

Lots of them.

All filling up the tunnel.

All approaching.

It was in that instant that Hayden realised exactly what this tunnel was now. Exactly what its purpose was.

It was a trap.

It was a trap, and he was stuck in the trap.

Stuck in the trap as the zombies got closer.

Stuck in the trap with only one direction to go.

Closer to the city.

Closer to the other side.

Closer to the very place this terrified couple were running from.

CHAPTER THIRTY-NINE

There was nothing else for Hayden to do but get up and run.

"Quick," he shouted, sprinting towards the terrified duo.

He couldn't see their faces. Not properly, not in this darkness. But he knew from the gasp of the man, Paul, that he'd startled them.

"We need to get back. Back towards the city. We need to get back there."

Hayden kept on running, not waiting for Paul and Shelly to follow. He could hear the zombies staggering ever closer. He could hear them snarling. Hear their footsteps thumping against the cold, damp ground. Smell blood and taste death in the air.

But all he could do was run.

All he could do was wait for Miriam and Sam to pull through with their end of the plan.

All he could do was hurtle on towards the city beyond the wall.

Towards the new world.

"You—you can't go that way," Shelly mumbled. "You can't go back there."

"You're wrong. We can."

"You're from outside. You haven't—you haven't seen that place yet. You haven't seen what they do. To people like us."

Hayden knew Shelly meant by "people like us." Outsiders. And although he didn't know exactly what they did to outsiders within these walls, he had an idea. He'd seen the depths of cruelty humanity sank to when its back was up against a wall. "I don't know exactly. You're right. But we can't... we can't stay here."

Hayden heard the small crowd of zombies closing in on Paul and Shelly, their silhouettes impossible to make out at this distance in the dark.

He heard the sobs of Paul. The sobs of Shelly.

He knew he couldn't go back for them. Going back was suicide. Going back meant deviating from the plan.

Then he remembered the boy.

He remembered the little boy looking back at him, desperation in his eyes.

The little boy he'd left behind...

No.

He couldn't leave these people behind. He couldn't leave anyone behind. Not anymore.

Because nobody was more or less important than anyone else.

Everybody was human.

Everyone deserved a chance to survive.

From outside or inside, everyone deserved a chance.

Hayden stopped. Ran back towards Paul, towards Shelly. He felt insane as the echoing groans of the undead danced off the walls and the ceiling of the tunnel. Felt like he was running into oblivion. Running towards an inevitable, unstoppable fate, reality slamming into him like a freight train.

He was going to die.

He was going to die...

No.

No, he wasn't going to die.

He was going to save these people.

And even if he did die, he'd die saving these people.

Die giving them a second chance.

It wasn't long before Hayden reached Paul, Shelly. He put a hand on their shoulders. The zombies were just feet away from them as they stared back.

"Quick," Hayden said, pulling them away.

But they didn't.

They stayed put.

"Come on!"

Shelly turned. Shook her head.

"There's nothing for us back there," she said.

The zombie at the front of the crowd snapped its teeth, hurtled closer.

Towards Shelly.

"No. That's not true."

Hayden lifted the wrench.

Swung it across the neck of the first zombie.

Split it apart.

He pushed past Paul, past Shelly.

"You go back there," he said. "You run to the gates. I'll be there soon. Try not to draw any attention. Try not to let anyone know I've survived it."

"How do you know you'll survive it?"

Hayden turned. Faced the ten-strong crowd of zombies, head on. "I will."

He swung the pipe against the neck of the next zombie.

Then slammed it through the decaying throat of another, hoping he'd got a clean hit, impossible to tell for definite in the blackness.

He attacked the rest of the zombies. Attacked them in this perfect darkness. And as he swung and stabbed the wrench at his victims, Hayden didn't recognise himself. He didn't recognise the man he'd become. The man he'd turned into in just a few short months.

The man he'd become in order to survive.

No. Not just to survive.

But to help others.

To help everyone he could.

Because that's what this world was about now. Not self-interest. Not hiding behind makeshift walls. Not rounding up the weak and hiding them away in prisons under nicer fucking names.

It was about helping each other. It was about starting again. But not from the top down. From the ground up.

It took Hayden a moment to realise the tunnel had gone silent.

Blood rolled down his arms. He could taste it on his lips. The wrench had bent, twisted, chipped at the top where it'd come into contact with a few too many spines. All his weeks of training. All his weeks of building his strength to survive this world alone. All of it going to better use.

He could see that now.

He wasn't alone.

He wasn't going to be alone.

Not anymore.

Not while there were people to help.

People to save.

People to survive with.

He turned around. Ran away from the fallen corpses of the zombies. Some of them still wriggled around, gargled, as he'd failed to take out their necks. And some of the ones whose necks he'd broken were still active, too. He didn't know why. Didn't know what other secrets the virus had. How else it'd morphed.

Only that it hadn't morphed in one way.

It hadn't morphed in the way the people running things behind this wall wanted everyone to believe.

He ran. Ran towards the city. Hoped Paul and Shelly were still fine. Hoped they were still okay.

A light flashed in front of him. Sudden, out of nowhere. It illuminated the tunnel. Too large to be a basic torchlight. Like a proper lantern. Expensive, undoubtedly. Heavy duty.

Hayden covered his eyes. Squinted ahead. Peered into the light. He tried to see beyond it. Tried to make out a sign of life. A sense of who was there. Who was watching him.

And then he heard a voice.

"Sorry about this. But it's time for the people beyond the fences to really, really understand what's happening to the people outside."

Hayden heard a click.

Then a blast.

CHAPTER FORTY

Hayden heard the blast of gunfire crack through the tunnel.

His instinct was to jump. To throw himself to the right. He wasn't sure how successful he was dodging the bullet. Wasn't sure how good an aim his enemy had on him.

Only that he had to jump.

He had to avoid being shot.

He couldn't just allow himself to be shot. Not now.

He fell to the ground. Got a face full of dust, a mouthful of blood.

He looked up. Saw the beaming light still shining at him. He couldn't feel any pain other than the pain of his fall, so he assumed he hadn't been shot.

Not yet.

He heard the gunfire again. Rolled to the right. Because that was all he could do. Roll. Fucking roll and hope for the best.

He hit the wall at the side of the tunnel.

The searing light closing in on him.

The man with the gun stepping closer.

"Why are you doing this?" Hayden shouted.

The man stopped. Hayden hadn't seen his face yet. Just the light. Just that bright light beaming down on him.

"Why am I doing this?" the man asked. There was a slight foreign twinge to his voice. Spanish, perhaps. "I'm doing this to protect our people."

"No. That's not true. You know as well as anyone we're not a threat—"

"This'll be easier if you're silent," the man said.

Hayden looked to his left. Looked into the darkness. Then he looked to his right. Looked over at the city. The entrance to the city. He couldn't see it. Not clearly. The light in his eyes was way too bright, distorting his view of everywhere else.

Hayden spat a lump of bloody saliva onto the ground. Looked back into the light. "There's people out there. Good people out there."

"I'm not doubting that."

"Good people who just want to survive. Who want to survive more than anything."

"But sometimes survival means making sacrifices. It means making the tough decisions. The difficult decisions. You are a part of that. Don't you see? You are a part of the greater future."

Hayden stayed still. He wasn't sure where Paul and Shelly had got to. All he knew was that they'd run in this direction. He hoped they were safe. He hoped, whatever happened, they'd made it someplace safe.

He hoped Miriam was safe.

He hoped Sam was safe.

"Then do what you have to do," Hayden said.

The light lowered.

Lowered, for just a moment.

Hayden took a deep breath.

Made the most of the moment.

He swung his right leg. Whacked it right into the man's left shin. Hard.

When the man lost his balance, Hayden dragged himself up. Threw himself at the man. Pushed him down to the ground.

The man continued firing his gun. The gunshots so loud they were ringing in Hayden's ears, chiming in his skull.

He pushed the man's right hand away. Pushed it down. Head-butted him, busting his own nose in the process.

He did it again.

And again.

Until the man's hand loosened.

Until his grip on the gun gave way.

Hayden snatched the gun from the man's hand.

Took the light from his left.

Shone it down on his face.

He saw the man. The olive-skinned man with the dark, curly hair. The brown eyes.

He saw the blood all over his face.

His bust lip.

His swollen eyes.

And he knew he'd done this.

He'd done it because he had to.

"Now it's my turn to apologise," Hayden said, heart racing, well aware of the one thing he had to do, the one action he had to take.

He pressed the gun into the man's chest.

"No, please!"

The man didn't say another word.

Not unless you count screaming as a word.

Hayden fired the bullet right into the middle of the man's chest. Felt his blood trickling down between his fingers.

And then he stepped away.

Shone the light on the man.

Shone it on him as he struggled.

As he writhed in agony.

As he whimpered.

He wanted to put him out of his misery. He wanted to finish him off, end his pain.

But he knew there was something else to do.

He knew there was another purpose behind his decision to shoot the man.

Another reason.

Hayden wasn't sure how long he crouched there in the darkness, shining the light on the man.

Shining it at him as he spluttered up blood.

As his eyes glazed.

As his skin greyed.

And he wasn't even sure whether he was in the right. He wasn't sure whether his suspicions were correct.

Just that he needed to know.

He needed to see it for himself.

See the same thing that'd happened to Anthony.

See the same thing that'd happened to Bob.

To Harold.

To so many others.

He'd almost given up hope when he saw the man's left hand twitch.

Hayden's heartbeat sped up. He could be wrong. Could just be a trick of the light. Could be looking at things the wrong—

Then the man's head twisted to the left.

His jaw snapped.

A bloody, throaty gargle emerged from his throat.

Hayden crouched there. Partly stunned. Partly in disbelief.

But mostly relieved.

Relieved, because his suspicions were true.

Relieved, because his hopes were right.

He wasn't a carrier. There was no airborne virus.

This was all a construction. All a construction by the people in power.

All a method of selective infecting.

With bullets. With injections. With knives. With God knows what else if it somehow got to little Tim. Maybe Tim just cut himself. Or maybe he'd ingested something. He didn't know. Maybe he'd never know.

But as he watched the man rise to his feet, blood still rolling down the front of his body, Hayden knew what mattered more than anything right now.

What mattered was the truth.

This gun had infected bullets in it.

The gun that shot Anthony had infected bullets in it.

The people behind the fences, running the camps, were using the infection as a weapon.

He lowered the gun, reached for his wrench, and went to swing it at the neck of the man.

Before he could, Hayden heard gunfire.

He watched as blood spurted out of the man's neck.

Watched his head snap to one side.

Watched the undead life seep from his body.

Watched him tumble to the ground.

He stood there. Silent. Listening to the echoing gunshot. Watching the blood roll out of the man's neck.

And then he heard the sound of shutters lifting to his right.

Felt fresh air drifting into the tunnel.

He turned.

Saw a mass of people standing at the entrance to the city.

Saw the look of shock in their eyes.

The look of bewilderment.

The look of fear.

At the front of the group, a number of well-armed guards, all dressed in black.

And in front of those, a man.

He was short. Wearing a black suit. Dark brown hair thinning at the sides. A look of remorse on his face, but the staged sort.

Like you often saw on television chat shows or reality TV before the world collapsed.

He was looking right at the fallen man. The man who Hayden had shot.

"And now you see," the man said, his voice a perfect RP intonation. "Now you see what happens when a carrier comes into contact with one of our own."

And Hayden understood.

Hayden understood what the man was saying.

How the man was twisting this situation in his favour.

The angry voices in the crowd lifted.

The frustration built outside the tunnel.

"We don't need to witness any more violence this evening," the posh man said. "Losing Luis in such circumstances is enough. Take him out."

CHAPTER FORTY-ONE

"Wait!"

Hayden wasn't sure where the voice came from. Somewhere within. Somewhere deep within him. A place that had more courage than he thought he had on the surface.

But as he shouted the word, he noticed he hadn't been shot. He noticed the men with the guns had indeed held their fire. That they were, in fact, waiting.

He looked at them. Looked at them, the dim lights of the city glowing behind them. He looked into the terrified faces of the residents. Of the confused looks. They looked like they'd been through hell. Like they'd seen all there was to see.

And Hayden hated to have to pull the wool from over their eyes. He hated to have to be the one to send their world crashing around them once again.

But he had to try.

"You can shoot me or you can at least listen," Hayden shouted, his voice echoing against the tunnel walls. "To what I have to say."

Silence from the crowd. A growing redness in the face of the main man, the posh man in the suit.

Hayden lowered the wrench. Pushed it away. And then he lowered the gun. Lowered the gun he'd shot the guy called Luis with. The gun that turned Luis. Just like the gun that turned Anthony.

"I don't want to threaten you. I don't want you to think I'm just walking beyond your walls to cause trouble."

"Murderer!" someone shouted.

"If it wasn't for you my son would still be alive!"

Hayden nodded. Swallowed a sickly, bloody lump in his throat. "I understand you hating me. I understand that. But you need to realise something. And that something is... is that we're all people. We're all humans."

"But you aren't welcome!" a man shouted from the back of the crowd.

"Maybe so," Hayden said, his voice croaky, his throat sore. "And I can understand that. I can accept that. I was like you once. I was holed up in a camp of my own. Worried about leaving. Worried about letting anyone else in. And rightly so. People killed the ones I loved. Not zombies, people. People have hurt me way more than the zombies have since the world fell. But it doesn't have to be that way."

A few mutters amongst the crowd. A few whispers. The air inside the tunnel getting colder, Hayden shivering.

"I respect your resolve," the main man said.

He cleared his throat. Pulled a white mask over his face. Stepped towards Hayden.

"I should introduce myself. Terrance. Terrance Schumer. I run this place. I run the world beyond the fences."

Hayden's fists tensed. He wanted to speak his mind. He wanted so desperately to speak the truth. *So you're the one who makes the decisions. You're the one in charge.*

"Mr Schumer," one of the guards said. "You might want to be careful—"

"It's okay," Terrance said, raising a hand. He looked Hayden right in his eyes as the light from the guards and crowd behind illuminated the tunnel. "I can handle this. We can talk this one out with dignity. Can't we, Mr..."

"Hayden. Hayden McCall."

Terrance Schumer stepped closer to Hayden. The crowd watched with wide eyes. Puzzled eyes. Terrified eyes.

"Mr McCall, I appreciate your concerns. But you saw it for yourself. What happened to my associate, Luis. That happened directly as a result of your carrier status. Just like the outbreaks in our city this evening. All as a result of migrants. You can understand our need to quarantine, can't you? You can understand our need to be careful?"

Hayden had to bite his lip to stop himself exploding with anger. "The people outside the fences. The ones you gunned down. Do you call that being careful?"

Terrance Schumer looked at Hayden with eyes even glassier than a zombie's. "I don't know what you're talking about. Whatever happens outside our fences is beyond our control."

So there it was. The lie. The lie to add to the ever-growing collection. Not only was Terrance Schumer lying to his people about the presence of an airborne virus to perpetuate fear of outsiders, but he was also lying about his people's involvement outside the walls, too. Lying about the preventative measures they were taking. "And what about Salvation?"

Terrance's eyes narrowed. "Sal... Salvation?"

"You know what I'm talking about. The camp. All the camps you have set up outside these fences of yours."

"Again, you must be mistaken."

"Mistaken. Right. Of course. I must be."

A long silence stretched on between Hayden and Terrance. And the longer it went on, the more the eyes of the crowd burned into him, Hayden knew he was going to have to do something drastic. Something subtle, but drastic. He couldn't blow it. He couldn't blow his reason for being here. His motive.

He had to play this right.

If there was a way of playing it right at all.

"You know, I will walk away," Hayden said. "Because I do believe in what you're getting at, ultimately."

"And what am I getting at?"

Hayden swallowed. "That sometimes sacrifices have to be made to preserve the wider society. That sometimes... sometimes people have to die to keep the majority alive. Sometimes, the weak have to pay to keep the privileged living."

Terrance didn't show any signs of responding to Hayden. Just frowned at him. Squinted, like he was weighing him up. Trying to figure him out.

"But I also believe in something else," Hayden said.

Silence, again.

Silence until Terrance opened his mouth.

"And what's that?"

Hayden took a deep breath in. Tasted blood on his tongue, sweat on his lips.

He looked past Terrance Schumer. Looked at the crowd of people. All watching. Waiting for an answer. Waiting for something.

"I believe that you've been lying to your people about the virus being airborne."

A shift in Terrance's demeanour. A slight turn to the right. "I... I don't know what you're—"

"I believe you've been intentionally infecting people. To terrify your citizens. To keep the powerful alive."

Terrance looked back at the onlooking crowd. Muttering picked up amongst them. More confusion. More bewilderment. "I... I don't know what you're—"

"And I'm going to prove it," Hayden said.

He took in another deep breath.

Then he crouched down.

Picked up the pistol.

He heard the command. Heard the panic in Terrance Schumer's voice. Heard the anxious cries of the crowd.

And he felt the first bullet hit him. Heard it hit him in his left shoulder. Send him tumbling back against the cold ground of the tunnel. Hot. Searing.

But Hayden clutched hold of the pistol.

Clutched hold of it, lifting it to his chest, the pain in his left shoulder getting stronger, stronger...

Lying on his side, Hayden put the gun to his shoulder. And he saw the look in Terrance Schumer's eyes as he started to run. Saw that look of realisation in his eyes. Of what Hayden was doing. Of what this was.

With the little strength remaining in Hayden's lungs, he said, "If I'm not lying, then let's just see what happens to me."

He closed his eyes.

Pressed the pistol to his own chest.

Pulled the trigger.

CHAPTER FORTY-TWO

Eliza Wisdom watched the man called Hayden fire a bullet into his own chest.

She held the rifle. Pointed it at him. Stood in front of the crowd of New Britain citizens like the rest of the guards and kept her aim.

And she heard the command. Heard the command from Terrance Schumer. The command as he ran back towards them, terror in his eyes. The command to fire.

But she couldn't.

She found herself standing there with her finger on the trigger of her rifle unable to fire.

Because of what Hayden said.

"If I'm not lying, then let's just see what happens to me."

Something about those words sparked a chord inside Eliza. She'd worked as one of the wall guards for months now. She'd been there when the fences were erected—when the tunnel was undergoing its rapid construction. She was proud of her home. Proud of where she lived. Proud of the future she stood for.

An inclusive future. A future for everyone.

But recently, there'd been incidents. Events that'd made her consider whether she was on the right side. First, there was Daniel. The way Luis shot him to the ground on Terrance's orders. And then the way he'd turned into one of those monsters later that night. Terrance insisted it was because he'd been exposed to the airborne infection. It was because he wasn't wearing his mask correctly.

But Eliza couldn't help but wonder.

She couldn't help but question.

"Guards!" Terrance shouted, panting as he jogged back towards the entrance to the city. "Fire! Put him down!"

The fact that none of the other guards beside Eliza had fired their weapons spoke volumes. Eliza turned. Looked at Martin on her left. Looked at Rajesh on her right. All of them holding their guns. All of them pointing their weapons ahead.

But that same look on their faces.

The look Eliza knew she must have too.

The look of uncertainty.

Of questioning.

Of wanting to see what was happening.

Of wanting to see what really happened to the man called Hayden McCall.

The man who claimed the group behind the fences had been infecting people all along.

Innocent people.

Refugees.

People needing shelter.

"Are you deaf? Do I need to repeat my command?"

Eliza shook her head as Terrance stepped in front of her.

"No," she said. "You don't."

She lowered her weapon.

Looked at Rajesh, into his bloodshot eyes.

He sighed. Lowered his gun.

Martin soon followed.

Terrance stared back at them, face reddening, blinking rapidly. "You... you are supposed to follow our orders."

"Why don't we see if he turns, just like he says he will?"

"He's a threat," Terrance said, speaking in hushed tones now. "He—he's a carrier. He poses a threat to—"

"Then let's just see what happens to him. Let's just see whether what he says about the bullet is true."

The crowd behind were quiet now. Silenced, like the realisation was setting on their minds too. Maybe Eliza was wrong. Maybe her suspicions were all wrong. Maybe she was opening the gates to the onset of infection. Airborne infection.

"You're putting everyone at risk. Just by standing here, you're putting everyone at risk."

"Then so be fucking it!" someone shouted.

A voice from behind. From the back of the crowd. And slowly, surely, Eliza heard a chant emerging. A chant accompanied by claps. The claps of the crowd.

"We want to see! We want to see!"

All of them were cheering now. All of them applauding. Like they were waiting for something. Egging Hayden on to turn, as miserable as it was. Because not only was he an innocent man, he was a good man. A man who'd sacrificed himself to free everyone else from the fear of the airborne virus. Who'd shot himself in the chest to show humanity that there was another way. A way beyond the fear. A way beyond the fences.

A way beyond Terrance Schumer's lies.

Terrance looked around at the crowd. His eyes were vacant, like he couldn't believe this was actually happening. Like he couldn't accept it.

But it was.

It was happening.

And these people were going to see.

As the chant went on, as the claps were accompanied by stomps, these people were going to see.

They were going to...

Movement.

Movement from Hayden.

The crowd quietened. Whispers emerged once more. The whispers that always signalled the fear. The fear of the outside that Terrance Schumer had been stirring for so, so long.

Not for long.

Not anymore.

Another twitch of movement from Hayden.

And then another.

Not proof.

Not proof until somebody saw it for themselves.

Until they looked the man in his eyes and saw how vacant they were.

"You don't know what you've done," Terrance said, voice cracking, shoulders slumped.

"We do," Eliza said, pushing past him, leading the crowd into the tunnel, away from the confines of safety, away from Terrance Schumer's imaginary boundary. "We've just finally grown the courage to see it for ourselves."

The crowd ran towards Hayden.

Ran towards his twitching body.

Ran towards the truth.

Towards hope of the truth.

Towards...

Hayden felt the strength drifting out of his body.

He rolled onto his back. The taste of metal intensifying in his mouth. A coldness covering his skin. At least he couldn't feel the pain in his chest anymore. Or the pain in his left shoulder.

All he could feel was a warmth.

A warmth inside him that felt familiar.

A warmth that, for some reason, made him think of Mum. Made him think of Dad. Of Clarice. Of Annabelle.

A warmth that made him think of Sarah. Newbie. Holly. Miriam. Of everyone he'd travelled with. Of everyone he'd cared for.

Everyone he'd lost.

Above all, as the chanting voices approached, Hayden thought of the boy. The little boy in the window. Except he wasn't afraid of him. Not anymore.

The little boy was smiling at him. Saying something to him.

Something like, "It's okay."

Something like, "I forgive you."

Hayden heard the footsteps getting closer and he closed his burning eyes.

Smiled.

Remembered what Bob said.

What he told him about people.

"People. That's what matters. Doesn't matter whether we're out here or behind a wall. What matters is we're together. That we're confident. That we fight."

And Bob was right. Miriam was right.

People were the most important thing in this world right now.

Togetherness was the most important thing in this world right now.

And in a way, Terrance's logic was right, too.

Sometimes sacrifices did have to be made to save others.

But not the kind he'd made.

Not for self-preservation. Not out of fear.

But out of ambition. Out of growth.

Hayden felt the life seeping out of his body, felt tingling sensations working up his arms, down his neck, his spine, the back of his legs, and he heard his older sister Annabelle ask him something clearly in his mind.

Did you do the right thing for other people?

For the first time, Hayden could only answer with one word.

Yes.

The warmth burst through his body.

Hayden saw his family clearly, right ahead of him, getting closer to him.

Smiling.

Happy.

He smiled back.

Then, nothing.

CHAPTER FORTY-THREE

Terrance Schumer watched the chaos unfold from a distance.

He saw the mass of people—his people—walk down the tunnel. Saw them move towards Hayden McCall. He'd shot himself. He'd shot himself with the infected bullet. Which meant he'd turn. He'd turn and expose the plan. He'd reveal the truth.

Specks of rain started to fall from the dark sky above. There was silence in the city behind him. Like the people who hadn't left their homes were waiting, holding their breath. Waiting for an answer. Waiting for some kind of sign.

But they didn't have to wait much longer.

The man that was once Hayden McCall twitched.

His head lifted. Shaky. Tensed.

And although it was still quite dark inside that tunnel, Terrance Schumer saw Hayden's eyes.

Saw the glazed greyness staring into nowhere.

Saw the blood rolling down his chin.

Heard the guttural grunt from the back of his throat.

Every muscle in Terrance's body went weak. Because now he had to explain. Now he had to explain why Hayden had turned.

He had to try and convince these people that it was nothing to do with the bullet. That—that carriers just turned when they were shot. That the rules were different for them.

But as the monster that was Hayden dragged itself to its feet, Terrance saw the crowd of his guards, his people, turn. Look at him. He saw the look in their eyes. Saw the hate. Saw the confusion.

"I—I can explain. I can explain everything."

Silence. Silence from the crowd, but for Hayden. Stomping towards the group. Blood rolling from the gunshot wound in his skinny chest. Teeth snapping together, hungry for their first flesh meal, like a horsefly in breeding season.

Terrance Schumer took a step back. 'Cause he knew right now that there was no reasoning. There was no arguing. These people had made their minds up. They'd seen the truth.

The worst part is they'd believe it.

They'd believed the truth.

The facade was over.

Terrance turned around. Started to run.

He stopped almost immediately.

In the street ahead—the street lined with the blood of fallen migrants—Terrance saw people outside their homes. Saw them walking towards him. Some of them with children in their arms. Migrant children they'd saved from the purge.

Some of them with weapons in their hands.

Knives.

Baseball bats.

Anger in their eyes.

Terrance stumbled back. Looked over his shoulder. Saw the people emerging from the tunnel. The chatter and the anger rising.

"Fucking liar!" someone screamed.

"Murderer!"

Terrance Schumer wanted more than anything to fall into a

hole in the ground. Because he'd made a mistake. He'd screwed up. He'd fucked up big time.

"I—I just wanted to keep us safe," he said.

And as the angry footsteps of the crowd approached, as the swarm surrounded him, Terrance Schumer really believed his own words.

He'd just wanted to keep his people safe.

Safe from outside.

Not just the zombies. But the trauma that came with it. The impact it had on the minds of the survivors from outside the fences.

From reality.

He crouched down in the dirt.

Closed his eyes.

Held up his hands.

"I just wanted to keep us safe."

The last thing he heard was the roar of the surrounding crowd.

The last thing he saw as he peeked through the cracks in his eyelids was a baseball bat swinging towards his face.

And then the inevitable blackness surrounded him.

CHAPTER FORTY-FOUR

"I'm telling you. Ain't a chance the guards are just gonna let you through the wall. Ain't a chance."

Miriam listened to the whiny voice of Garth, the guard they'd thrown into the back of the truck, as she drove back towards the fences. It was pitch black. Rain fell and hit the windscreen, a case not helped by the dodgy wipers in this heap of shit. Outside, in the glow of the flickering headlights, Miriam swore she saw movement. Movement of zombies. The undead watching them with their empty eyes. Finding a new source of movement to follow.

But they didn't matter. Not now.

What mattered was the wall.

The wall that was just a matter of metres away.

Miriam turned to her left. Saw Sam sitting upright in the passenger seat. Cute kid. So well behaved, too. Considering everything he'd been through. All the shit a kid like him must've witnessed in a world like this.

"How you holding up, kid?" Miriam asked.

Sam glanced at her. His infectious little smile grew across his gaunt face. "I'm okay."

"You sure about that?" Miriam asked. She never held herself in high regard when it came to talking to children. She was okay at talking to teenagers. Fine at playing with babies. Her sister Penny had twin boys two years back, and in the wake of the breakdown of her relationship with Kelly, Miriam found a lot of comfort in spending time with them, looking after them.

But kids Sam's age. Just after the baby stage, well before the teenage stage. They were tricky to talk to. Like frigging aliens.

"Well, I..."

Sam shook his head. Smiled again. "It's okay."

Miriam slowed the vehicle as they got closer to the wall. She thought about quizzing Sam more. But she knew how that'd look. Like she was prying. Like she was forcing an answer out of him. She knew how much she hated that herself. Always used to get right on her tits when Mum asked her how she was doing. Of course she wasn't doing well. Not when she knew Dad was sleeping with his secretary from the office. Not when she'd caught them in bed together. Then in the shower.

But what did she say to Mum? What did she tell her?

Miriam took a deep breath. Refocused on the tunnel ahead. The fences were wide open. Nobody was around. She wasn't sure whether that was a good or a bad sign.

"I'm telling you; they're gonna be out lookin' for me. And when they find me in here, they'll make sure a shitload of people are at the fences. They'll be waiting for you. I'm tellin' you. There's no way out of this. Just—just let me go and we can call it quits."

Miriam looked back at Sam. Caught him smiling. She smiled back at him.

"We'll see about that," she said.

Then she accelerated into the dark tunnel, past the fences, towards the city beyond.

Miriam drove slowly through the tunnel. She didn't want to risk being ambushed. But she couldn't deny the strange feeling she had. The sense that nobody was watching. The sense that something had happened. Like she was heading into a ghost town.

She squinted beyond the range of her headlights towards the city. She couldn't see anything. No opening. Nothing like that. Just darkness. Just total darkness.

Maybe Hayden was still in here. Maybe he was trying to find his way into the city.

Or maybe he was...

She felt something under her left tire.

Felt the truck elevate as it drove over something.

For a moment she worried. Had she hit Hayden? Shit. She didn't think she was going quickly. Surely she'd have seen him. Surely she hadn't just hit him.

And then she saw the bodies in the headlights.

There was blood. A lot of blood. Bones poking out of flesh. Vacant expressions. Twisted necks.

The fear kicked in again. Hayden. What if Hayden was amongst them? What if Hayden had been bitten by them?

"Look. Someone's there."

Sam's voice snapped Miriam out of her thoughts.

She raised her head. Saw him pointing out the windscreen.

Through the windscreen, in the glow of the headlights, Miriam saw the outline of a figure. A man. About six foot one in height. Short hair. Skinny.

She saw him standing there and her heart fluttered. Hayden. It was Hayden. He was okay.

And then she saw the way he waddled towards the truck.

Saw the way he put one foot in front of the other. Unsteady. Uncoordinated. Like a toddler.

"Is... is it dead?" Sam asked.

Miriam swallowed a lump in her throat, nasty tastes building up in her mouth.

She wanted to move. Wanted to get out the truck. Wanted to see him. See him for herself.

But she couldn't.

She couldn't get out because getting out meant accepting it.

Accepting the truth.

Accepting the reality.

It wasn't long before Miriam had to accept reality anyway.

Hayden stood in the headlights. Pale-faced. Blood oozing from his chest, his shoulder. His eyes pointed in two directions. But they weren't looking at anything in particular. Not really.

She saw him and she felt her own eyes sting.

She saw him and she knew he'd failed. She knew they'd both failed.

She knew what she had to do.

She put a hand on Sam's arm. "You wait there a sec. I won't be a minute."

"But I'm scared—"

"Just, please. Wait there. Please."

Sam stared at her for a moment, uncertain.

Then he nodded.

Miriam reached for the pistol. It felt alien in her hands. Out of place. But she knew that was because of what she had to do with it.

Of the act she had to commit with it.

Again.

She saw her mum in her mind. Saw her screaming as Dad dragged her across the kitchen floor. As he wrapped his teeth around her ankle. Chewed down on her Achilles, blood spurting all over the new cream curtains.

She saw Dad committing his final sin against her mum.

And then she'd lifted the gun.

Fired.

Put him down.

Put Mum down too.

Just to save her from her eventual misery.

To save her from her pain.

Miriam stepped out the truck. Dropped down to the tunnel floor. She tightened her grip on the pistol handle. Listened to the rumbling engine of the truck.

Then she heard the groan.

It was awful. Shiver-inducing. Mostly because she could recognise it. Recognise it as Hayden's voice. That was the worst part of the groans. They always held a trace of the person they once were. Always a reminder that they were once alive. And now they were nothing but an empty shell.

Nothing but a cry.

Miriam took in a deep breath of the musty air.

Listened to the water dripping down from the tunnel roof above.

Then she turned towards Hayden.

Turned into the light.

Hayden was just a few steps from her. Dragging his left foot along behind him. His neck was tilted to the right. His teeth were cracked from all their snapping.

She looked into his eyes and hoped he'd see her. Hoped he'd recognise her. For who she was.

But she knew that wasn't going to happen.

She knew that was never going to happen.

Not to anyone.

She lifted her shaky hand. Pointed the gun at his neck. She turned away at first. Felt a warm tear rolling down her cheek. She'd pretended not to like him. Tried her best not to get too attached. But she knew he was a good person underneath all his fears. She knew he wanted what was best for everyone. Just that all his hope had been buried. Buried and charred by this god-awful world.

He was a leader. He wanted the best for other people.

"I'm sorry it didn't work out," Miriam muttered.

She watched as Hayden staggered closer. Just five steps away now. So close that he could just reach out. Grab her. Rip her throat away.

And maybe that'd be for the better. Maybe death was the best option.

No. That was bullshit. She had Sam to look out for. She'd made it this far.

She had to keep fighting.

She couldn't give up.

And that meant doing what she had to do.

She looked into Hayden's eyes again. Looked into them and remembered the first time she'd seen him. Fearful. Lost. But prepared. Prepared to help her escape the Salvation prison. Prepared to help her make it this far.

Just afraid to lose anyone.

Afraid to lose anyone else.

Afraid to lead.

"You... you got us this far," Miriam said. "I'll never forget that. I'll never forget that."

She heard Hayden's snarl echo against the tunnel wall.

Watched him lunge towards her.

Squinted.

Squeezed the trigger.

"You don't want to do that," someone said.

Miriam stopped. Moved out of the way of Hayden. Watched him fall face flat on the tunnel floor.

She looked back. Looked back from the direction she'd come. Back into the darkness. A woman. She'd heard a woman. She'd...

A group of people were walking her way.

A group of people led by a woman.

Hayden snarled once more. Stuck his fingertips into the dusty concrete and forced himself upright, his body twisting and contorting in impossible angles.

Miriam watched the woman and her group get closer.

There were more of them. Way more of these people than she first thought.

All walking so confidently.

All walking so... fearlessly.

Hayden looked right at the woman. He was just feet away from her. Inches, even.

"Watch..." Miriam started.

But the woman just brushed past Hayden.

Her people just brushed past Hayden.

He didn't notice them.

He didn't even look at them.

Miriam's heart raced. She couldn't understand. Couldn't understand what this was. What was happening. Whether this was some kind of dream. Some kind of twisted reality.

Then the woman stopped in front of her.

Illuminated by the light.

She was dark-skinned. Short. Old, probably in her fifties. She had a serious expression. A serious expression that scanned Miriam's face like she was trying to see inside her; read her soul.

And then Miriam became aware of the people around her. Men. Men in... in black suits with crosses around their necks. Women in the same outfits. And with them, a box. A wooden box on wheels. Diamond covered. Six people at the back of the group dragged it along. Walked past Hayden's zombie like he wasn't even there. No regard for him, none whatsoever.

"What... who are you?"

The woman stared Miriam right in her eyes.

Scanned her a little longer.

Hayden growled again. Started stumbling towards Miriam.

"Restrain Hayden. We're going to need him."

A few of the men grabbed Hayden by his arms. Held him back. He kept on lifting his feet, trying to walk, unaware of their restraints, unaware of anything but Miriam, but fresh meat.

A sudden shiver crept up Miriam's spine. "Wait. Hayden? You... you know his name?"

The woman's glaring gaze softened. She half-smiled.

"I know a lot of things, dear. A lot of things indeed."

She held a hand out. Behind her, Hayden continued to snap, continued to writhe, continued to struggle.

Nobody seemed to care.

"My name is Martha. And I'm here to share some very important news."

CHAPTER FORTY-FIVE

Terrance Schumer felt the rough concrete underneath the soles of his bare feet and knew there was no escaping his new reality.

He walked. The afternoon sun was baking hot. The warmest day of the year by far. Not a cloud in the blue sky.

Just typical. Like the gods above were laughing at him. Like they too were punishing him for the things he'd done. For the actions he'd taken. For the lives he'd cost.

He looked ahead at the long, ever-stretching road. It used to look distant from up in his tower where he was most comfortable. But out here, out here on the other side, it dragged on even further. Every step just stretched on and on. Danger lurked behind every unmanned car. Beneath every partly open manhole cover. Over the top of the embankments beside the road.

The weight on his back didn't help.

He tensed, dragging his package even further. The package they'd attached to his back. The people who'd forced him out; forced him away. Told him to take it with him. Take it with him and get it out of sight. To take it far away, where it was nothing more than a memory. A dark memory of events that'd unfolded in New Britain.

A reminder of what he'd done.

A literal weight on his shoulders.

A weight he couldn't escape even if he wanted to.

The sickly stench of rot came to him in droves. Reminded him of what he was dragging along. Of what he was carrying with him. He tried not to look back at it. Because it brought back too many memories. Too much guilt.

He just had to get somewhere safe.

One of his old prisons. Lock himself in a cell.

Or get to a town. Somewhere where somebody would take him in. Because that's what he needed. Refuge. Forgiveness.

But the package attached to him would never go away.

The taste of death pumping around his taste buds would never go away.

He heard something. Heard a shuffling over to his right. He turned. Caught a glance of the package behind him. Heart racing. Sweat dripping down his head, the sun beating down, muscles weak.

He looked over the embankment. Looked over to where he'd heard the shuffling.

Nothing.

He took a few deep breaths. Closed his burning eyes. All in his head. Just a figment of his imagination.

Had to keep on walking.

Had to keep on moving if he wanted to survive.

Had to—

And then he heard the shuffling again.

This time, from directly behind.

His body froze. The pain in his shoulders intensified. The pain he was doing everything he could not to focus on.

He clenched his teeth together.

Turned around.

The first thing he saw was the package.

And when he saw it, he felt that wave of nausea, that wave of realisation, hit him again.

Attached to his back by six solid nails into his skin, into his muscle, glued and stitched back in place, was a net.

Inside that net, remains.

Remains of people he'd killed.

Remains of the refugees he'd had butchered in the street.

Loose heads of children.

Arms poking out the side.

The smell intolerable.

Flies swarming.

But he didn't focus on the package for long. Not this time.

Because all he could focus on were the three figures behind it.

The three figures approaching it.

Slowly.

Terrance turned around. "Fuck." He moved a little faster. Not much faster, but as fast as a man with a bunch of human remains tied to his back could manage. He knew he was leaving a trail of blood behind. He knew he was walking bait.

But he had to keep moving.

He had to get somewhere safe.

He had to...

He saw the movement up ahead and stopped in his tracks.

In the distance, four more figures. All of them staring at him blankly. Not making a noise yet, but watching him. Heads twisting in the air. Like they were sniffing at it. Trying to weigh Terrance up.

He stood there, totally still.

Then, when the first of the zombies groaned, Terrance made a break for the embankment hill.

He collapsed onto it. Tried to drag the package up the grassy slope. It was too heavy. Way too heavy. No chance he was getting up there with this on his back. No chance he was getting anywhere with these nails in his skin.

He looked at the nails rammed into his left shoulder. Looked at the congealed blood underneath the glue, between the staples. He saw his skin going purple. Saw puss seeping out. If the dead didn't get him, infection would.

But fuck it. He'd rather take a chance with infection.

He reached his hand over. Grabbed the first of the nails. Just touching it sent burning agony through his body.

He clenched his teeth together. So hard he felt them going wobbly.

The groaning mass of zombies edged closer.

Terrance stuck his fingers into his skin. Ripped away the staples, each one of them splitting away making his head throb, his consciousness drift.

But no. He had to keep on going. As fresh blood trickled onto his right hand, he knew he had to keep on going.

He cut through the glued skin with the tips of his bitten-down fingernails. Got a grip on the head of the nail.

Felt tears rolling down his cheeks as the growls edged ever closer.

He held his breath.

Gripped the nail tighter.

And then he pulled.

The pain wasn't so bad. Not at first.

Not until the nail got about halfway out of his shoulder.

And then he couldn't help but scream. Couldn't help but cry out.

Yet still, he kept on pulling.

Still, he kept on ripping the nail from deep within his flesh.

Blood splattering down his arm, onto his neck.

He got a grip of the next nail as he pulled it away. His pulse blasted through his skull. He felt cold. Icy cold. And he knew what was happening. He was going to die. He was going to pass out and he was going to die.

He'd never wake up.

No. No, he would wake up.

Just not as himself.

Not anymore.

He yanked the nail further out of his flesh, well aware of how on the brink of death he was.

Something different happened this time.

The nails came free of his skin.

The rope dropped to the ground.

He looked down at the bunch of nails. Looked at the sinewy pink flesh clinging onto their rusty exteriors. His head spun. His muscles were weak. But he had to keep on going. He could make it now. Now the nails were free he could make it. He could...

A sudden sickness hit him square in the middle of his chest.

He still had to get the nails out of his right shoulder.

He turned. Looked at the wound where the nails were slammed in last night. Sweat poured down his face as memories of the last extraction swirled around his mind.

The pain.

The dizzying agony.

He couldn't do it.

He couldn't...

No.

He had to.

He took a deep breath.

Put his shaking, blood-soaked fingers on the head of the nail.

And then he heard the grunt.

Right above him.

He looked up. Didn't want to, but nothing he could do about it. Nothing he could do to control it.

He saw the decaying face of the first zombie.

A man. Ginger. Five foot something.

And a blonde woman. Thin hair. Chunks of her scalp dangling loose onto her face.

And more of them, too. A whole crowd of them. All of them staring down at Terrance. All of them groaning.

Terrance let his grip of the nail go.

Smiled.

Wiped the tears from his cheeks.

And as the zombies surrounded him, he knew what this was.

Justice.

Justice for the people he'd let down.

Justice for losing himself in self-interest, self-preservation.

Justice for—

He didn't have any more thoughts.

Just agony as the zombies sunk their teeth into his body.

Ripped the flesh from his bones.

Tore him to pieces in the blazing sun.

CHAPTER FORTY-SIX

Shelly Bellamy took a deep breath of the warm summer air as she walked through the New Britain Park.

It was an afternoon, and a beautiful one at that. Inside the park, which had just recently been reopened, Shelly saw families. Families with their children by the pond, feeding the ducks. Families playing with footballs. In the distance, families throwing frisbees to one another.

Happy families.

Hopeful families.

She listened to the sound of the laughter and felt a warmth inside as well as out. The smell of freshly cut grass. The whiff of the hot dog stalls, making her salivate at the thought of delicious cooked onions.

She used to be able to close her eyes tight and convince herself she was still in the old world. Before everything went to shit.

Now, she didn't even have to close her eyes.

She just had to keep her gaze away from the fences.

That was enough.

She walked down the pathway past a young couple on one of the benches. They smiled at Shelly, and Shelly smiled back at them. There was a gratefulness about the place since Terrance Schumer had been ousted. Since word of his lie spread. Using a weaponised distribution of the virus to keep people out of New Britain, to keep the fences filled with the kind of people he wanted here.

Xenophobia. Engineered fear.

But that was all gone.

That was all different now.

Shelly walked through the middle of the tall oak trees. She could see the memorial in the distance. The memorial had only opened three days ago, marking three months since the Great Shift—the name they used for the transition of power from Schumer to the Wider Council. Shelly had been too busy looking after Paul to visit. He'd been sick. Not infected sick, no, but getting skinnier and skinnier for weeks now.

But he was feeling better today. He was feeling perkier. So Shelly figured it made sense to get some fresh air herself.

She saw the memorial up ahead as she waded past the last of the trees. Saw the headstones in the ground. But most of all, more than anything, she saw the tall rock in the middle. The tall rock dedicated to the man who'd made the greatest sacrifice of all. The man who'd put other people ahead of himself. The man who'd shown New Britain what leadership really was.

Hayden McCall.

She stopped when she saw Miriam beside the memorial. She didn't know Miriam all too well. Just that she got on well with Hayden. Something between them.

She looked absorbed in her thoughts. Like she didn't want to be interrupted. So Shelly turned and started to head back to another section of the memorial.

"Jeez. You scared me then."

Shelly stopped. Turned. Saw Miriam looking at her.

She was wiping her bloodshot eyes, but she was smiling.

Shelly nodded. "I can… I can give you some time. If you—"

"Time? God no. I've spent more than enough time at this place." Miriam backed away from the memorial stone. "Shelly, right?"

Shelly nodded. "Miriam?"

"That's the one. So. What d'you make of what they've done here?"

Miriam observed her surroundings. The headstones. The names etched into them. Some of them left anonymous, for the people who'd sneaked in, who died unknown. "It's... It's nice. A good tribute."

"I think it's a bit fucking creepy if I'm completely honest."

Shelly couldn't contain herself from smiling. "I suppose it is."

A pause in speech between them.

"He was a good man," Miriam said, breaking the silence. "Not... not to piss on everyone else's parade. But he deserves this statue. Deserves this memorial."

Shelly nodded. She remembered the moment Hayden convinced her and her husband to flee back towards New Britain that very night they were trying to escape. "He saved my life."

"He saved all our lives," Miriam said. "And for that I..."

She stopped. Her voice broke. Fragility in her tough exterior.

She looked back up at the statue, wiping away her tears. Took an audible deep breath. "I thank him. Because I see what he did now. I thought he'd failed. I thought we'd all failed. But he didn't. He didn't fail at all. He did exactly what he had to do. For all of us."

Shelly looked back at the tall rock. Looked at Hayden's name etched into the concrete. "He's loved by a lot of people."

"You got that right," Miriam said.

Her voice broke again. She exhaled. Looked down at the grass.

"Say, do you fancy a beer?"

Shelly smiled. "I... I guess."

"Seems weird asking that question even though it's been three months since 'normal' came along. Right?"

"Right."

Miriam smiled. Walked away from the memorial stone. Shelly walked beside her.

"I don't know how long this'll last," Miriam said, as they exited the park, the fences looming large around the outskirts. Manned by guards. Guards to take out the oncoming zombies. Guards to let people inside. Guards to control the future.

"But I'm not sure it even matters right now," she said. "As long as we've got 'right now'. That's the most important thing."

Shelly inhaled the sweet summer air deeply.

Listened to the sounds of laughter.

The sounds of happiness.

The sounds of normality.

And then she walked away from the park. Away from the memorial. Towards the city. The normal city. The new reality.

Hayden McCall's sacrifice never left her mind.

Hayden McCall's sacrifice never left anyone's mind.

BACK AT THE BELLAMY HOUSEHOLD, Paul coughed up blood.

DEEP IN THE LABS, outside of view, He heard a muffled voice above. A woman's voice. A familiar voice.

"He's awake."

WANT MORE INFECTION Z?

The fifth and final book in the Infection Z series is now

If you want to be notified when Ryan Casey's next novel is released (and receive a free book from his Dead Days post apocalyptic series), please sign up for the mailing list by going to: http://ryancaseybooks.com/fanclub Your email address will never be shared and you can unsubscribe at any time.

Word-of-mouth and reviews are crucial to any author's success. If you enjoyed this book, please leave a review. Even just a couple of lines sharing your thoughts on the story would be a fantastic help for other readers.

For a full up to date list of all the author's books, head over to this link: http://ryancaseybooks.com/books

Printed in Great Britain
by Amazon